Rachael Thomas

———

NEW YEAR AT
THE BOSS'S BIDDING

HARLEQUIN PRESENTS®

Recycling programs
for this product may
not exist in your area.

ISBN-13: 978-0-373-13879-1

New Year at the Boss's Bidding

First North American Publication 2016

Copyright © 2016 by Rachael Thomas

Printed in U.S.A.

www.Harlequin.com

They were snowed in. Xavier and Tilly were alone.

His body still hummed after the exchange between them that morning. A carnal need so strong had filled him as he'd looked into her vivid blue eyes. He'd had to resist the urge to crush her to his body, to feel her against him and to kiss those seductively plump lips. Never before had he felt so untamed, so in danger of losing his renowned self-control.

Now, because of the weather, he was going to be forced to spend at least the next twenty-four hours with a woman he desired more than any other, one who'd made it known she was unattainable, here to fulfil a contract, nothing more—a contract which expired at midnight.

He knew she wouldn't be comfortable about being alone with him this evening. Not after that moment in the dining room. She was not his usual type of woman, more the forever sort, and that held him back. Forever was something he couldn't do, which was another reason for not exploring what was between him and Tilly.

He took a deep breath, bringing all his wayward desires under control, determined to shake off his inconvenient lust and be the perfect gentleman—until midnight at least. He returned to the kitchen to break the news to the only woman in the past three years who had threatened to rouse the man he'd once been, the man he could never risk being again.

"It appears we will be here alone for New Year."

Rachael Thomas has always loved reading romance and is thrilled to be a Presents author. She lives and works on a farm in Wales—a far cry from the glamour of a Harlequin Presents story—but that makes slipping into her characters' worlds all the more appealing. When she's not writing or working on the farm, she enjoys photography and visiting historic castles and grand houses. Visit her at rachaelthomas.co.uk.

Books by Rachael Thomas

Harlequin Presents

From One Night to Wife
Craving Her Enemy's Touch
Claimed by the Sheikh
A Deal Before the Altar

Visit the Author Profile page
at Harlequin.com for more titles.

NEW YEAR AT
THE BOSS'S BIDDING

To editors Laurie Johnson and Charlotte Mursell. Thank you so much for your fantastic support, guidance and encouragement as I've moved from unpublished finalist in SYTYCW 2013 to this, my fifth book.

CHAPTER ONE

TODAY NOTHING COULD dampen Tilly Rogers's enthusiasm for the exciting contract she had landed. Tonight she would be catering for Xavier Moretti's New Year's Eve dinner party, a contract that was a much-needed boost to her new business.

The manor house he'd hired for the occasion, set on the edge of Exmoor, was proving difficult to find, but even that didn't faze her. She was away from London and thankful that this New Year's Eve would be very different from last year's.

Tilly gripped the steering-wheel of her small white van a bit tighter as the light flurry of snow landing on the windscreen increased to a constant bombardment of small fluffy flakes. She must be almost at the manor by now. At the next turn in the road she was relieved to see a large set of wrought-iron gates loom ahead of her, but that relief soon faded.

The gates were firmly closed and she looked down the long drive. No sign of the manor house, but on one of the tall pillars 'Wimble Manor' was proudly announced. She was in the right place.

Judging by its grandeur, this must be the main entrance and from her brief conversation with the caretaker she knew that, as hired staff, she needed the back entrance. Slowly she pulled away, aware of the snow beginning to settle on the tarmac road ahead of her. Thank goodness she'd left London earlier than planned.

A little further along she saw a small gate-house. A set of open gates nestled in the winter-bare hedgerows and she turned in, following a set of tyre tracks that were just still visible on the now white driveway. Someone else had just arrived, but it couldn't be her staff, Katie and Jane. They weren't due until later this afternoon, by which time she hoped it would have stopped snowing.

Cautiously she drove along the snow-covered lane, but couldn't resist a glance around the grounds of the manor, which were turning, very quickly, into a winter wonderland. The narrow road led through a small wood, over an old stone bridge and on the other side, Tilly got the first sight of Wimble Manor.

'Oh, my goodness,' she said as she looked up at the imposing manor house. The snow, now blowing horizontally, gave it a mysterious air, filling her head with romantic notions of the house in its heyday. If only she had time to take a walk, but that was a luxury she couldn't afford. Tonight's contract was one she had to get right. As undisputed king of the motorcycle racetrack, who'd turned businessman and mentor for young riders, Xavier Moretti was her most high-profile client to date.

The email asking her to take on his New Year's Eve dinner party had been a shock, to say the least. Not only was it just what her fledgling business needed, it was also what she needed on a personal level. It would provide her with a welcome distraction from dwelling on what had happened last New Year's Eve and created the perfect excuse for not attending parties.

Although her best friend, Vanessa, had complicated things when she'd told her she planned to announce her engagement on New Year's Day so she couldn't completely escape the party scene. After last year, Vanessa had been anxious but Tilly had reassured her she was over it all now. She knew that whatever happened she would be at the party to prove this to herself as well as her friends. It would be part of reinventing herself, just as starting the business had been.

She dragged her mind away from thoughts of engagements and parties and focused on Xavier Moretti's request for authentic Italian home cooking, something she really wanted to specialise in after the hours she'd spent in her Italian grandmother's kitchen as a young girl. She smiled at the memories, determined to make this evening's meal so special he and his guests would remember her name for a long time.

Thoughts of the menu she was going to present them filled her mind as she followed the narrow driveway around the side of the impressive house and into a courtyard. She noticed the tyre tracks also went this way and assumed it was the caretaker preparing for Xavier Moretti's arrival. She hoped that wouldn't be too soon. She had planned on having the morning to herself, giving plenty of time to prepare for the New Year's Eve dinner.

Lost in her thoughts, she didn't register that the tracks belonged to a sleek black sports car, now partly covered in snow. She parked alongside it and got out, totally in awe of her surroundings. She looked around the courtyard, her face upturned as she took in the grand house, not caring about the white flakes as they landed on her skin and settled in her red woolly hat.

She pulled her scarf higher around her neck and resisted the urge to cross the cobbled courtyard and see what was in the other buildings. There would be time enough for that later. She had a van to unload and a kitchen to set up. There was still a lot of work to do ahead of tonight's dinner party and with a regretful sigh she turned then stopped, as if suddenly frozen by Mother Nature herself.

In the open doorway stood a man, so tall, handsome and self-assured she was certain, from the internet pictures she'd seen, it was Xavier Moretti. He watched her with an expression of confidence and, if she wasn't mistaken, amusement. A hint of a smile lingered at the edges of his lips.

His dark hair lifted slightly in the wind, the odd white flake settling starkly against the midnight blackness of his hair before dissolving away. His tanned complexion looked totally out of place against the backdrop of England's winter weather and she could hardly drag her gaze from him. He looked so exotic with a hint of wildness that she found strangely exciting.

Unused to being in the company of such a man, she struggled to regain control as she blushed, her stomach fluttering with what felt like excitement. On a newly discovered level, she knew it was more than that and fought hard to ignore it. She had to remain professional with this man, no matter what. This was the first time he'd hired Tilly's Table for a dinner party and she needed more contracts like this to help her business grow, not to mention the validation his custom would give.

He had certainly dressed for the part of country gentleman. The dark grey sweater, over a blue shirt looked warm and casual. Alarmingly, she couldn't quite stop her gaze sliding down his long jeans-clad legs. What was the matter with her? She'd never lusted after a man. Ever. Finally gathering her way-ward reactions, she looked at his face, saw his stern dark eyes watchful.

'Hi, I'm Tilly Rogers and here to cater for Mr Moretti's dinner party this evening.' His increased smile did little to help the fluttering feeling but confirmed her suspicions. This was Xavier Moretti.

'*Buongiorno*. Xavier Moretti,' he offered,

his heavy accent making the words far sexier than she'd ever heard any man sound, and the Italian greeting nudged at memories. 'I had not expected the pleasure of your company so early, Ms Rogers. Tell me, do you always find such joy in snow?'

A tingle of pleasure skittered down her spine, setting off alarm bells. What was happening to her?

'It's so nice to be out of London.' She couldn't keep the enthusiasm from her voice. 'But I didn't expect you to be here yet, Signor Moretti.' She wouldn't allow him to dampen her spirits—or spoil the plans she'd had of exploring once she'd finished her preparation.

'Xavier, please.' He shrugged nonchalantly. 'You should come in and get warm.'

'I'm fine.' She shook her head and smiled, trying to ignore the tingle that continued to zip down her spine at the deep sexy tones of his voice. 'Besides, I have things to bring in so I can start work.'

He crossed the snow-dusted yard to hold the back door of the van open as she leant in to grab the first of several boxes. As he took the boxes from her, his fingers brushed hers. The sizzle that shot up her arm made her eyes widen and, unconsciously, she looked at him.

The depths of his dark eyes held hers and for a moment it was as if time had stood still. As if nothing else in the entire world mattered.

Her heartbeat seemed to slow and just the simple task of breathing became difficult. His handsome face didn't give anything away. He looked composed and controlled but still she couldn't break whatever it was. All she wanted to do was look at his high chiselled cheekbones, as if doing so would allow her to commit them to memory before locking the image behind a door labelled *Danger*.

Why had she thought that? She was definitely out of her depth, but a man like him would never look twice at a woman like her. She averted her gaze, using the pretence of checking the contents of one of the boxes to divert his attention.

'May I help?' The three words held a hint of huskiness and to her dismay she blushed again, her stomach fluttering as he took the boxes inside. She watched him walk away, thankful she could think and breathe properly again.

She pulled more boxes from the back of the van and followed him into the house. 'I hope this snow stops,' she said as she walked into the kitchen, where Xavier was stacking her things on a large table. She needed normal conversation to settle herself. How could he un-balance her so quickly?

'*Sì.* But you are here at least. It would have been a shame not to sample your food, espe-cially as it has come so highly recommended.'

Tilly blushed, this time because she didn't know how to deal with such a direct compli-ment, or was it guilt at having those wildly im-proper thoughts about him just moments ago?

To cover her embarrassment, she put her boxes down and turned to survey the massive kitchen. From the stainless-steel pans hanging above the range to the copper moulds mounted on the walls it managed to combine perfectly the charm of past with the needs of the twenty-first century.

'This place is amazing. I'm really looking forward to working in such a grand kitchen.' Her enthusiasm for the old house couldn't be subdued and for a moment he watched her, coolly assessing her and everything she did.

Tilly scanned the high-ceilinged room, wishing she had a kitchen like this to work in for every job she took on. Sleek, modern kitch-ens, packed full with every gadget, were what she was normally provided with, but this room, with history breathing from its walls, practi-cally filled her criteria for a perfect workplace.

'*Si, è bello,*' he said, as she turned her attention back to Xavier.

Did he have to keep using sexy snippets of Italian? It tugged at bittersweet memories of happy times she'd spent in a small cottage kitchen in Tuscany, where herbs had dried in abundance and the warmth of the sun had seemed to shine constantly.

When she went back to her van, the flurry of snow she'd arrived in had dwindled to almost nothing. Only the odd rogue snowflake whirled to the ground. At least that was one thing less to worry about.

As she leaned into the van she moved aside the dress she'd bought for Vanessa's engagement party tomorrow. Her heart hadn't been in that task, but she didn't want her past to spoil her friend's happiness. She paused and touched the black dress through the plastic cover, remembering the wedding dress she should have worn exactly a year ago. The conversation she'd had as it had hung on her wardrobe door filtered unwittingly back from the past. The firmness of Jason's voice still reached her as he'd told her he needed much more than just friendship, urging her to go out and experience life—just as he planned to do.

Pain and humiliation rushed through her.

She couldn't do this now. Looking back wouldn't help. With a sigh, she pulled the last of her boxes towards her and turned to see Xavier come out of the house, his expression serious as he looked up at the heavy grey sky, before swiftly returning his attention to her.

'Please, allow me,' he said, as she tried to close the back of her van as well as balance the boxes.

'Thank you.' Shyness crept over her again. She didn't like the way he managed to fluster her or the sensation as his fingers innocently brushed over hers.

'Prego.'

There it was again, that undeniably sexy voice speaking in a language she'd known as a child, when her grandmother had shared all her cooking secrets with her, unwittingly sealing Tilly's future career.

Tilly shut the van doors, leaving her overnight bag and dress inside, determined she would be at her friend's engagement party tomorrow. Especially when Vanessa had been so supportive last New Year's Eve—the day her world had fallen apart. She couldn't deny her friend happiness, even if it opened up the agony of what should have been her wedding day. A year ago today had been the day her engagement had ended—the day her childhood sweetheart had said he no longer wanted to marry her.

Irritated that memories of last year could still hurt, she made her way back to the kitchen. Xavier was standing against the range cooker, looking so relaxed he might as well have been in his own home and not an English country house he'd hired for the occasion. She placed the final box on the kitchen table, aware of his dark gaze watching her every move, feeling it with every sizzle that sparked down her spine.

Xavier leant against the warmth of the range, which reminded him of his childhood home, and watched as Tilly unfurled her scarf and pulled off her hat. Her thick blonde hair looked ruffled, stirring visions of her in his bed after a passionate night. This unexpected thought raced through his mind all too clearly, sending a stab of lust through him.

The instant attraction he felt for her was inconvenient. He'd hired her company for his New Year's Eve dinner after she'd been recommended, but not once had he considered that he'd find the owner of Tilly's Table so attractive.

It must be this house, being in a different

environment, one so similar to the warm and loving environment he'd grown up in. It was giving rein to inappropriate thoughts of the owner of Tilly's Table. She was attractive but completely unaffected by it—a totally refreshing concept for him. Being in this house with such a down-to-earth woman, a woman who'd want a forever kind of love, reminded him his eventual aim had been to settle down and be happy. But that was no longer possible. The accident three years ago had slashed those hopes.

'Would you like coffee?' Her sweet voice, which he couldn't help but notice sometimes held a hint of mischief, dragged his thoughts back to where they should be. As did the reminder that his parents, his cousin and her husband would soon be here.

At least they would keep his mind on the enforced New Year celebrations, although he still found it hard to accept they had coerced him into it. He knew they were upset and worried that he hadn't celebrated Christmas with them for the last few years, but it was a time of year he now hated.

Tilly pulled off her puffy black coat, revealing her slender figure encased in tight jeans and equally well-fitted black roll neck jumper. They showed every curve to perfection, dragging him from dwelling on the past and back to that unprompted vision of her in his bed.

'*Grazie*,' he replied, as he fought with the maelstrom of emotions that scenario provoked.

What was the matter with him? He wasn't usually this easily distracted by a woman. His attention had been caught by Tilly Rogers that first second he'd seen her. What man wouldn't be attracted to such a beautiful woman? But he'd never been this aware of a woman within minutes of meeting. He'd never seen his now-futile hopes of happiness dangled before him so temptingly.

Already he knew she was a breath of fresh air, compared to the usual women who lived in the circles he was now moving in since arriving in London. Beneath Tilly's smiles and laughter he sensed a vulnerability that echoed his, calling to him and drawing him inexplicably towards her.

She'd clearly set the boundaries—professional boundaries—addressing him by his surname, but he couldn't help wishing they had met in another way. Or was it his rebellious nature, wanting what was so obviously denied him? Whichever it was, he wanted more, something he found hard to deal with.

Belatedly he realised it wouldn't make any

difference. He would have needed to have met her before the accident. No woman, not even a warm and genuine woman like Tilly Rogers, would want to be involved with him now, not once the truth came out. The scars on his legs were a constant reminder that he didn't deserve to be happy, that he was the one with ideas above his station, which was exactly why he hadn't done anything more than have dinner or go to a party with a woman for the last three years.

He sensed her watching him as he walked towards the kitchen windows and looked out into the courtyard. Why did he suddenly want things that were no longer possible? Things Carlotta's reaction had forced him to deny himself? He'd seen her look of revulsion after the accident, had known she'd blamed him, and had ended it right there and then, guilt making anything else impossible. He didn't deserve happiness after what he'd done.

'I forgot some files,' she said lightly, and reached to pull her keys from the pocket of the coat she'd laid over the back of a kitchen chair. 'I'll fetch them now.'

He watched her walk to the back door, her boot heels tapping a gentle rhythm on the tiled floor. The sway of her hips mesmerised him as if he were a teenager who'd just discovered the delights of women. He shook the haze of desire away and went to the back door to assess the weather.

He hoped it would stop snowing soon, aware his family would be convinced he'd purposely hired such a remote venue in the hope it would snow, releasing him from entering into the spirit of the season for yet another year. If he was honest with himself, escaping such gatherings was why he'd remained in England, extending his scholarship programme instead of going back to Milan and concentrating on his motorbike factory.

Tilly turned and smiled, her eyes sparkling. 'It's a shame the snow has stopped. I was hoping to see the countryside covered in a white blanket.'

He looked up at the heavy grey clouds that held the promise of more snow. 'You may yet get your wish.' He would then escape the torture of celebrating New Year's Eve, of pretending everything was normal, when it never would be again.

'Do you think so? It's not forecast,' she said, as she unlocked her van and lifted out a red file, the innocent excitement in her voice made him laugh gently. 'I haven't seen real snow for so long, only icing-sugar dustings. There was nothing when I left London.'

'I grew up in the hills of northern Italy, where snow is a regular feature of winter. I think we will see more snow today, the sky is heavy with it.' If they had been in his home in Italy, they would most certainly be snow-bound, a thought that served only to heighten his awareness of her.

'That would be fun, but only after your guests have arrived.' She laughed lightly as she reached into her van again. He gritted his teeth—hard, catching a glimpse of creamy flesh as her jumper rose up. He really must stop thinking of her like this. Just when he'd thought he couldn't take any more she straightened and arranged the files in her arms, but didn't seem able to meet his gaze. Did she feel it too? This sizzle of attraction? Did she have any idea what she was doing to him?

'I have work to do and I'm sure you do too.' If he didn't remove himself from her company, he might be tempted to breach the boundaries of professionalism before she'd been here for more than an hour. The urge to take her in his arms and kiss her was completely overwhelming and something he hadn't thought of with any of his recent *dates*. 'I will show you the dining room and lounge first.'

Feeling like an ill-tempered bear who had been woken from his winter sleep, he stalked back into the house, aware Tilly was following. His footsteps sounded fierce on the tiled floor as he made his way to the main hall and staircase. Her gasp of pleasure drew him up sharply as he reached the stairs and he turned to look at her, pressing his lips firmly together in discontent as she looked around the large hallway, which showcased the Christmas tree he'd expressly asked to be removed before his guests arrived. Its decorated branches were yet another reminder of what he no longer deserved.

'This is so beautiful.' Clutching her files against her, she walked slowly towards the bottom of the wide staircase, where he stood. She stopped and looked around her at the magnificence of the main entrance of the manor. 'And this tree, it's just gorgeous. I always wanted a tree like this when I was young. Something grand and tall, but of course it never happened.'

The laughter in her voice held a hint of sadness and abruptly she stopped talking. Had his reaction to the mention of Christmas been that severe?

'Yes, the tree.' He gritted his teeth again, feeling even more like a grumpy bear, trying to ignore the longing in her voice. 'I did ask for it to be taken down before I arrived.'

'Take it down. Why? It's Christmas.' The shock in her voice was crystal clear but, then, she didn't understand that he no longer indulged in sentiments like that.

'It *was* Christmas.' The words were growled out as he pushed back emotions he still couldn't deal with. How could anyone come to terms with the knowledge that they'd caused an accident that had taken the life of a friend? His recklessness that day on the track had wrecked one family's Christmas for ever, depriving young children of their father.

She shook her head. Fast little shakes that made her hair move and glisten like gold beneath the hall lights. 'Christmas hasn't finished yet and you are celebrating New Year here.'

'I'm entertaining my family. Nothing more.' He didn't want to take this any further and turned towards the dining room, leaving her little choice but to follow. She'd only been here a short time and already she was disturbing the inner peace he'd thought he was finally beginning to achieve, threatening to open up wounds that had only just started to heal.

'This is where I will entertain my guests this evening.' He stood back as she entered the large and stately room, the long table capable of seating at least ten people taking centre stage.

She stood quietly next to him but he could tell she was desperate to walk around the room, touch the old furnishings and feel the ambiance of the place. He stifled a smile as she took out her notepad and pen, using the cover of efficiency to hide that fact.

'It's a very big table. How would you like it set for this evening's dinner? At one end, perhaps closest to the fireplace?' She looked up at him and he felt as if he'd been caught out as his study of her had been blatant. For a moment her eyes searched his, questions lingering in hers, and a flush of heat coloured her cheeks, something he found quite endearing.

'*Sì*, by the fire is good.' He moved away from her and the temptation she represented, but he couldn't stop watching her.

As she wrote down notes, he enjoyed the way her hand moved fluidly across the page. With her head bent, her blonde hair slid off her shoulder, forming a curtain of gold. He itched to reach out and push it back, wanting to see the concentration on her face, to feel it with the stroke of his hand across her skin.

She looked up at him suddenly, her eyes locking with his, and questions surfaced once again in the summer sky blue of hers. 'And the champagne? Perhaps here would be best?' She moved further away from him and he let out a breath he hadn't realised he'd held onto. He had to stop this.

Her footsteps were muffled on the carpet as he watched her walk towards the ornate sideboard, stopping to make further notes. Then she moved to the tall windows, her air of professionalism momentarily forgotten as an almost childlike joy shone from her. 'It's snowing again.'

Thankful for the distraction, he crossed the room to join her. As he stood behind her he realised just how small and delicate she was and a powerful urge to protect her washed over him.

He looked down at her at the exact moment she turned to look up at him. The warm blue of her eyes, which instantly reminded him of the Mediterranean Sea, drew him closer to her. He could smell her perfume, dusky roses, as it weaved around him, invading every part of him. The urge to lower his head and feel her full lips against his was so strong that he could actually taste her.

'I had better get started.' She ducked away

from him, leaving him looking out at the view.
What had just happened? He'd nearly lost control, nearly allowed himself to imagine things
that were no longer possible. He hadn't been
the same man after the accident and he had no
right to want any woman, especially this bubbly blonde—not in any way.

He couldn't risk hurting anyone else.

Tilly's heart pounded so hard she was sure
it must be echoing all around the old house.
For a brief moment she'd seen raw desire in
Xavier's eyes and had been convinced he was
about to kiss her. No, that couldn't be possible. An attractive and successful man would
only look past her, but she couldn't shake the
thought of him kissing her. Worse than that,
she'd wanted him to. The heady longing that
had engulfed her so rapidly still hummed inside her, shocking her with its intensity. She'd
never felt anything like this before. Was this
what Jason had wanted from her when in her
innocence she'd thought she could keep him
as a friend?

She almost groaned aloud. She didn't want
to think of Jason and what had happened last
New Year's Eve. She'd left London to avoid
doing that. Now Xavier Moretti, with his dark

and brooding attitude, which called to her on a level she hadn't known existed, opened all those memories up again for further scrutiny.

'I have made slight amendments to your menu requests,' she said officiously, desperate to regain control. She took in a somewhat ragged breath, trying to find her normal well-balanced sense of what was right and wrong. And wanting this man to kiss her was wrong. Very wrong.

'So long as it still remains mostly Italian, as I requested.' He strode across the room and she moved back away from him until she stood against the ornately carved chair at the head of the dining table, its solidness grounding her.

'I spent some of my early childhood in Tuscany with my grandmother. It's where my love of food and cooking came from, so I can assure you your menu will remain true to Italy.'

He stopped and looked directly into her eyes, his brows raised in question. Or was that shock? 'Your grandmother is Italian?'

'Yes,' she said, unashamedly proud of her heritage. 'She named me Natalie because I was born on Christmas Eve. My mother, however, preferred Tilly so it was only ever Nonna who used my full name.'

'Your surname is not Italian.' His accent had

become more pronounced, but his tone was firm and controlled.

'No, my grandmother married an Englishman, which divided the family, and my father was the only child of that love match. Then he married my mother, an Englishwoman, and they moved to London.' She began to explain, then realised he probably wasn't interested and that she'd better concentrate on work, instead of divulging her family history.

He took a step towards her and instinctively she moved back, pressing herself more firmly against the back of the chair, wishing he would leave and give her space to think, room to breathe. The effect he was having on her was unlike anything she'd ever known.

'In that case, I am looking forward to seeing your changes.' His accented voice had a deep sensual undertone, which only intensified the flutter of attraction she was finding hard to ignore.

'Thank you, I'm sure you will be more than pleased with them,' Tilly rambled, still confused by the way her body reacted each time he spoke or looked at her from those sexy black eyes. It certainly wasn't professional but it made her feel alive.

He continued in fluid Italian and she blinked

in shock. 'I'm sorry,' she said, as the usual sadness washed over her. 'I don't remember much of the language. Nonna died when I was only thirteen. My mother is English and although we did use Italian in the home, it wasn't very often.'

Sometimes she thought she must remember all those conversations with Nonna, that deep inside her they were waiting to come out. She just wasn't ready for that to happen yet, because that would mean going through all the heartache and loneliness she'd experienced since her father had died. She could see now that Jason had helped her even before their childhood friendship had moved towards engagement. He'd filled the large void in her life—until he'd found someone else.

Xavier shrugged in that sexy devil-may-care way he'd done as she'd stood in the courtyard and her heart rate began to accelerate once more. 'It is sad, no? When you have Italian ancestors.'

'Maybe one day I'll take Italian classes, or even go to Italy,' she said lightly, wanting to move on from this discussion. It made her think of Jason, their broken engagement and the vows she'd made to herself that day. That had been the beginning of her bucket list.

Things to do since she was no longer part of a couple. So far she'd only ticked off one, to start up her business and to provide for herself. The remainder, including finding her father's family, still called to her.

'*Sì*, you should do that.' He moved to the door and turned to look at her, his tall body framed by the dark wood surround. 'You shouldn't deny your past.'

'My past?' What did he know of her past? She'd always made sure her private life never crossed into her business. She didn't want people knowing about Jason jilting her hours before their wedding. It left her feeling vulnerable and she'd had enough of other people's pity.

'Your Italian ancestry.' He frowned and she realised her immediate leap to defensive mode had alerted him to something he hadn't even been aware of.

'Yes, you're right,' she said, and pushed her body away from the chair and walked towards him as he stood in the doorway. 'I will go to Italy one day.' It was on her bucket list after all.

He nodded his approval at what she hoped was a light-hearted comment and moved to leave the room. 'I have work to do before this evening and I'm sure you have things you need to do but, please, feel free to make yourself at home here.'

'Thank you, I will.' Shyness swept over her and she lowered her lashes. The thought of making herself at home here, as if she were a guest, made all sorts of improper images rush through her mind. She looked back up at him and blushed. His handsome face was stern and etched with control. It was hard to believe that only moments ago she'd thought he might kiss her. Or had that just been her fanciful imagination?

'*Mi scusi*, Natalie.'

Before she had time to remind him nobody had ever called her Natalie, except her grandmother, he was gone. She could hear him striding back through the hall at a fast pace, obviously wanting to relinquish any responsibility to her.

'*Grazie*, Xavier,' she whispered to the emptiness of the room, enjoying the feeling of Italian on her tongue. Then she shook her head vigorously against the longing to be kissed his look had ignited in her. Silly girl, don't even go there. He hadn't been about to kiss you.

From what little she knew of him from the internet she guessed he would be a playboy, a man who never dated a woman twice. He was not what she wanted. She wanted to be loved and cherished and to find her happy-ever-after. He was her client—nothing more.

But still her mind wandered back to the sexy Italian who'd just stalked out of the room. She looked at her watch, hoping that soon her staff and his guests would arrive. She wouldn't have any time for improper thoughts then.

She forced her mind back to the job she was here for and the preparations still to be made. The sooner she got them started the sooner she could finish and leave for the bed and breakfast she'd booked. Tomorrow she would go to Vanessa's family home, to a party that would test her ability to have moved on from last year.

She couldn't allow herself to become distracted by Xavier Moretti. He was not what she needed, no matter how charming and handsome he was.

CHAPTER TWO

TILLY DIDN'T DARE leave the dining room and wondered what had just happened. She lingered, hoping that he would have gone to do his work if she stayed for a while. She made more notes and plans for the dinner party and tried not to remember the moment she'd thought he was going to kiss her. It had terrified and excited her all at the same time.

Xavier Moretti was typical of men with wealth and power, using them to get what he wanted. But he had the added advantage of more sex appeal than was necessary. He must be used to just about every female he came across falling at his feet. She knew he was toying with her, flirting and using his charm just because he could, but she wouldn't succumb, she'd had enough hurt recently. But somewhere deep inside she was unnerved to realise she wanted to.

With this thought foremost in her mind,

she knew she couldn't hide away and made her way back in to the hall and towards the kitchen, smiling as she passed the Christmas tree. Whatever Xavier Moretti's problem was with it, she loved its bright cheerfulness. Moments before she entered the kitchen the smell of fresh coffee alerted her to Xavier's presence.

He was stood against the range cooker, looking disturbingly sexy. Or was that just the aftermath of her daydreams?

'Problems?' His dark eyes seemed to mock her thoughts, as if he knew she'd spent the last half an hour longing to know how it would feel to be kissed by him.

'No,' she replied, deciding that if she got straight to work he would probably leave. 'Sorry, I didn't mean to disturb you.'

'You are not disturbing me, *cara*. I was just making coffee.' His accent, together with the term of endearment, sent a tingle of awareness zipping through her and she grappled for something neutral to focus her mind on.

'It's still snowing.' The delight at the prospect of snow was now beginning to be replaced by unease, scrambling her thoughts. Or was it just being in Xavier's company?

'*Si*,' he said, his attention focused firmly on her, unsettling her as she opened her folder with the itinerary of all she needed to do ahead of this evening. 'But I'm sure the roads are clear. It looks worse than it is, with nothing but parkland surrounding us.'

'I certainly hope so,' she said quickly, trying to quell her panic over his mention of clear roads, something she hadn't considered when wrapped up in her newly created fantasy world. 'I have two members of staff due to arrive from London in a few hours.'

He didn't reply, but the heavy look in his dark eyes as he studied her left her in no doubt he'd heard her. She looked down at the pages in her folder, trying to make sense of the words, which seemed to dance on the page as her heart thumped hard. What was the matter with her? She'd never behaved like this over a man but, then, Jason and his calm, safe presence in her life was all she'd known. Since her early teens they'd been inseparable.

The fizzing excitement as Xavier's gaze met hers was something she and Jason had never shared. Could the lack of such intensity have been his reason for calling a halt to the wedding?

She still recalled the painful blow of his words as he'd told her he didn't love her, that he couldn't marry her because of a brief affair.

One that had made him realise there was more to life than waiting for her to be ready, and in a moment of daring rebellion she'd added *romantic fling* to her bucket list. Not only that, she'd told Vanessa, who constantly reminded her of it.

Now Xavier had made her examine things she'd finally begun to move on from. Angry he even had that power, she began opening cupboards, lifting out the pans and bowls she needed to start preparing tonight's meal. Now was not the time to think of Jason and it certainly wasn't the time to think of Xavier—in any way except as her client. It wasn't as if she was about to have that romantic fling with him.

'I'm positive they will arrive.' She glanced at him, the hint of amusement in his voice catching her attention. 'Just as I am sure my guests will also arrive. If we were at my home in the Italian mountains I would say that we are almost certainly destined to spend at least the next few days alone here.'

Romantic images of his home in Italy, mountains covered in snow, and spending time in front of roaring open fires with a particular sexy Italian rushed into her mind. 'Thankfully we are not in Italy,' she snapped, annoyed with herself for allowing such thoughts to manifest themselves so rapidly and vividly.

He laughed. A low slumberous sound that sent her pulse into overdrive. He dominated the kitchen, despite the capacious amount of space within the room.

'So the idea of being alone together doesn't appeal to you, *cara*?' His accent had become heavier as he looked at her intently, his eyes so black they resembled a starless night sky.

'It's not something I've considered,' she replied in a brisk matter-of-fact tone, and began to empty some of her boxes. She tried had to not think about it, not when there was danger is such thoughts. 'Now, if you don't mind, I have work to do.'

Xavier watched as Tilly arranged her things on the table with careful attention to detail. He couldn't help but smile. She *had* considered the thought of being here alone with him. Just as he had. He'd surprised himself by wishing they were at his home in the mountains, where once the snow started it would build up quickly, rendering them snowbound.

Rational thoughts kicked back in. If they were alone, truly alone, he wasn't sure he could ignore the attraction, which very definitely existed between them. Not to mention that time alone with her would inevitably mean she would learn too much about him.

His guilt and anguish about the accident would soon become evident and that was something he went to great lengths to conceal—even from himself. He hadn't spent one night with a woman since he'd banished Carlotta from his life the day after the accident. So why was the idea of being with Tilly becoming so appealing?

He looked up at the large clock on the kitchen wall. Just four more hours until his family arrived. He resented that they'd come all the way from Italy, forcing him to host the evening, challenging him to be the man he'd been before the accident. If it had been anyone else other than his parents suggesting they spend New Year's Eve celebrating, he'd have said no.

At least once they were here he would be safe from the temptation of this bright and bubbly blonde, the first woman who had tempted him since the accident.

'When do you expect your staff to arrive?' He hoped it was soon, because right now he wanted to kiss her, just as he'd wanted to in the dining room. He still couldn't comprehend that within less than an hour of her arrival he'd been forced to hold back the need to feel her lips beneath his.

That sort of loss of control was not him. He was calm and precise in all he did, paying attention to every small detail. He knew well enough exactly what one moment of recklessness could do. To want to kiss this woman was irresponsible in every sense of the word, but he liked to get what he wanted—and right now that was Natalie Rogers.

She glanced at the clock, then back at him. 'They should be here just after lunch.'

'Va bene,' he replied, as he moved towards the table and closer to Tilly, unexplainably drawn to her. She looked warily at him, reinforcing the boundaries she'd already subtly laid down. So why did he want to challenge and test them?

All he needed to do was avoid the kitchen until her staff arrived. If he locked himself away in the small lounge he'd chosen as his study he could finish the reports he'd brought with him and avoid giving in to the primal call this woman was making to him. It was something he'd never known before and adrenalin flowed through him, making him feel alive and powerful. Exactly the way he'd always felt sitting astride his bike at the beginning of a race, when the desire to win had been all that had mattered.

Not that he'd ever race again. Those days were over—finished by an accident which lingered in his mind by day and haunted his dreams by night. Instead he'd increased production at his bike factory in Milan and set up a scholarship school, touring Europe in the hope of teaching young riders to race safely.

His heart thumped and in his head unbidden memories lurked, threatening to overwhelm him. He leant on the back of a chair, waiting for the pain in his legs to pass, a constant reminder of the months he'd spent in hospital after the crash. He gritted his teeth against his anger.

For the last year he'd been free of moments like this—at least during the day. He knew exactly why it was happening again. Because it was Christmas. The time of year he thought of a family missing that one special person—the rider he'd brought down by his reckless riding. His friend, damn it.

A warm hand touched his arm. The feel of it through his shirt and cashmere sweater brought him back from the edge of the guilt-filled hole he'd been looking into, which had been threatening to drag him back into its hellish depths.

'Are you okay?' Tilly's soft voice, full of concern, hauled him back the rest of the way. He lifted his head and looked directly into her eyes, which were as blue as the sea on a summer day.

'*Sì*,' he growled and pushed back from the chair, severing the contact of her touch. He didn't deserve her sympathy. He didn't need her soft touch and concern. If she knew the truth, knew all the damning facts about the accident, she wouldn't be so quick to offer her compassion.

He sensed her draw back. Saw her step away, anxiously catching her bottom lip with her teeth, but still the anger and guilt he'd carried since the accident raged inside him. Tilly was doing exactly what Carlotta had done the first day she'd visited him in hospital— backing away in disgust. Carlotta had despised him because of what had happened. The unwritten message in her face had fuelled his guilt and anger.

'Are you sure?' Tilly's voice, hesitant and gentle, cracked the bubble of agony he was in, but anger at the vulnerability she'd exposed remained, tormenting and weakening him.

'Of course I'm sure.' The harsh words snapped from him ungraciously. He needed to get the hell out of here, before her concern tipped him over the edge and he submitted to the urge to confide in her about the guilt he'd carried alone for the last three years.

She didn't say anything but returned to her unpacking, apparently unfazed by his display of anger. She hadn't deserved that. He should apologise, but afraid that would make her question him further he stalked from the kitchen adamant he would remain out of Tilly's way for as long as possible.

Those painful memories began to subside, until he walked past the Christmas tree. He couldn't acknowledge Christmas, not any more, which was why he'd insisted the tree be removed.

All it represented to him was three father-less children facing another Christmas. His selfish desire to win had done that. It didn't matter that he hadn't been the only rider not to change tyres, not to heed the warnings of the wet track. None of that mattered, not when he thought of those children. Paulo's children.

With a heavy sigh he walked on towards the lounge he'd commandeered for the duration of his stay. Once the door was shut he allowed himself to give in to the guilt-laden memories of the day he'd smashed just about every bone in his legs and taken out his friend in the process.

He sat at the desk and turned on his laptop. Would he ever be rid of the horror of that day? Would the guilt that he'd survived ever lessen? He took in a deep breath and closed his eyes, refusing to let memories claim him.

When he opened them again he looked out of the old windows at the grey sky, each pane of glass forming a frame for the large flakes of snow that now fell in a swirling dance past the window. The quiet peaceful scene soothed him and eased the physical pain, reminding him of his happy childhood.

Tilly had worked frantically for the last hour or so, anxious she hadn't discussed fully the menu changes with Xavier that morning as planned, but his sudden change of mood had made it impossible. At one time he'd looked as if he'd been in terrible pain and instinctively she'd gone to him, only to have her concern hurled unceremoniously back at her.

Now more pressing issues dominated her thoughts. Where were Katie and Jane? They should have been here by now. Tilly walked to one of the three tall sash windows of the kitchen and looked out. Big flakes of snow were falling against the backdrop of a heavy grey sky. Not good. What if they couldn't get to Wimble Manor? How would she cope tonight on her own?

She grabbed her coat from the chair she'd left it on earlier and went through the passage to the back door. The heavy wooden door protested as she pulled it open and snow whirled in with a rush of cold air.

'Oh, my goodness.'

Her little white van and Xavier's sleek black car were nestled beneath a deep blanket of snow. The courtyard cobbles, which this morning had only been dusted with white, were now completely covered. A strange and heavy silence hung around the buildings as the flakes fell thick and fast. It should be peaceful and calming, yet the silence seemed to scream at her, as if warning of trouble.

'I don't think you should try going anywhere right now.' Xavier's accented voice broke through her turmoil and she spun round to look up at him.

'I hadn't planned to, but I do need my staff to be able to get here.' Panic returned as she wondered how she was going to manage without the girls. They'd become a practised team and had worked for her since she'd started Tilly's Table almost twelve months ago.

'Have you heard anything from them?'

'No, I'll check my phone.' Her words were sharp with exasperation at herself. Why hadn't she thought of that earlier? She'd seen the snow flurrying past the windows but had been too caught up in the excitement of preparing the meal—and avoiding the man who disturbed her equilibrium.

Irritated by his practical approach, she moved past him, back along the passage and into the kitchen. Unable to quell her panic, she lifted her paperwork and uncovered her mobile phone to see she'd missed Katie's call. With ominous dread settling as fast as the falling snow, she dialled into her messages and heard Katie's anxious voice explaining the roads were so bad they'd had to turn back.

Now what was she going to do? A five-course meal for Xavier and four guests was scheduled for this evening. She would have to be preparing and serving.

But what if nobody could get here?

'They had to turn back,' she said slowly, panic making her heart thump as he joined her in the kitchen. 'There was lots of snow, even around London, but it became worse the further out they got.'

Spurred into action, she tapped in a text to Katie, asking they let her know when they were back safely and not to worry about her. She was safe and warm at Wimble Manor. Xavier looked across the room at her and she wondered at the truth of that statement. She'd thought he'd been about to kiss her only a few hours ago and she had wanted him to. How safe was that?

'I'm not sure how I'm going to be able to give you and your guests the meal I'd planned,' she said firmly, resisting the urge to panic.

'Because you do not have staff to help?' The hint of humour in his voice snared her attention and she looked at him. The aggressive edge she'd seen earlier that morning had gone. The anger, which had given him a feral fierceness, smoothed away.

'I don't have any staff to serve. I had hoped to be able to concentrate on presenting the best meal possible.' She averted her gaze from his dark eyes and flicked through her folder. She would have to find ways to make it simpler but still remain a meal people would remember. What she presented this evening would be the shop window of her new business.

'And what if my guests are also unable to drive through the snow?' He leant on the table and looked at her as she bent over her files. His eyes locked with hers as she looked up and again that unnerving sizzle shot between them. Instantly she stood upright and backed away a step from the table.

'You mean nobody is coming?' Tilly froze and looked at him. They would be alone. Just the two of them?

'I haven't been able to contact them yet,' he said, almost too calmly.

'I think I'd better carry on. Just in case they can make it.' She spoke more for her benefit than Xavier's and began to make sure all the ingredients for dessert were ready.

As she did so, she felt his gaze on her and tried hard to ignore the spark of awareness rushing around her, tingling on her skin as if he'd touched her. He was her client. She couldn't and shouldn't be thinking of him like this. He turned his attention to making coffee and relief soothed the tremor of awareness he'd sparked.

Besides, he was so far out of her league it was laughable. He wouldn't be remotely interested in her and after Jason's sudden change of heart last year she really didn't want to get mixed up with another man, especially not one who ignited something unknown and passionate inside her. He definitely gave off warning vibes of danger.

Xavier placed a hot cup of expresso on the table in front of her and she looked up at him, unable to believe her train of thought. How had she not noticed this morning that he'd looked so dangerous, so wild and untamed? His slightly too-long hair wasn't as neatly combed back as it could be and his eyes were so black they sparked.

'Thank you.' Her voice had turned into a husky whisper and she wanted to look away from his intense eyes, but she couldn't. Her heart began to race and she was thankful that the table was between them, preventing her from moving towards him, from acting out the need to feel his lips pressed firmly against hers in a kiss so passionate it would take her breath away.

Where had that thought come from?

'*Prego.*' That one word sounded sinfully sexy and she dragged in a deep and calming breath. Just when she thought she couldn't stay beneath his hot gaze any longer he turned and walked away, leaving her so deflated she flopped down onto the nearest chair.

She listened to his fading footsteps, trying to calm the erratic thud of her heart. What the heck had just happened? Whatever had passed between them in those few seconds had not only been hot, passionate and explosive, it had also been wild and dangerous.

Xavier ended the call he'd just received and looked out of the window. Snow was still falling. Big thick flakes twisting with increased speed down to earth, building upon what lay on the ground after this morning's dusting. Neither his guests nor Tilly's staff could get to the manor and they certainly wouldn't be able to get out.

They were snowed in.

He and Tilly were alone.

His body still hummed after the exchange between them that morning. A carnal need so strong had filled him as he'd looked into her vivid blue eyes. He'd had to resist the urge to crush her to his body, to feel her against him and to kiss those seductively plump lips. Never before had he felt so untamed, so in danger of losing his renowned self-control.

Now, because of the weather, he was going to be forced to spend at least the next twenty-four hours with a woman he desired more than any other, one who'd made it known she was unattainable, here to fulfil a contract, nothing more—a contract that expired at midnight.

He knew she wouldn't be comfortable about being alone with him this evening. Not after that moment in the dining room. She was not his usual type of woman, more the forever sort, and that held him back. Forever was something he couldn't do, which was another reason for not exploring what was between him and Tilly.

He took a deep breath, bringing all his wayward desires under control, determined to shake off his inconvenient desire and be a perfect gentleman—until midnight at least. He returned to the kitchen to break the news to the only woman in the last three years who had threatened to rouse the man he'd once been, the man he could never risk being again.

Tilly was at the sink, her back to him as he entered, and he let his gaze linger for a moment then reminded himself of his decision of moments ago. Appreciating her petite figure wouldn't help him at all.

'It appears we will be here alone for New Year.' As he spoke she turned to face him. For a brief moment he saw shock in her eyes, which tugged at the defence of irritation and anger he'd shrouded himself in. He couldn't let her do that, for her sake as well as his.

'I was just watching the snow. I've never seen so much falling.' Her voice was very calm. She didn't sound disconcerted that they were to be here alone in this rambling country mansion. Her expression as she looked at him told a different story.

'My family are not prepared to travel as the forecast has changed. It isn't good. It seems tomorrow we are now due to have blizzard conditions.' He relayed the information he'd been told by his cousin, not wanting to panic her.

'I hope Katie and Jane get back okay.' She moved away from the window and to the table, where her food preparations were under way. 'I guess you won't need all this now.'

'The evening plans will remain the same,' he said curtly, not liking the way she nudged at emotions he'd thought had disappeared after the crash. He was beginning to feel a strange urge to care for her, protect her and keep her safe, but knew he couldn't, not when guilt and blame lay at his feet.

Her blue eyes widened in shock and a startled gasp left her lips, doing untold things to his already stirred-up senses. He clenched his hands into tight fists at his sides, resisting the urge to cross the room, take her in his arms and kiss her until she gasped his name in pleasure.

'But it will be just the two of us.' Her silky soft voice, which stumbled slightly over the words, did little to quell the mounting desire within him, as did the image of them dining alone. He'd promised himself he'd be a perfect gentleman this evening and, no matter how hard that was, he would do it.

'*Sì, solo noi due.*' Hampered by his loss of control, he reverted to Italian. He'd never been like this with a woman. Even as a young and inexperienced man, he hadn't floundered as he was now. It was a totally new and unwelcome sensation.

'You can't expect me to spend the evening with you. Not completely alone.' She frowned at him but still looked incredibly enticing.

'I can and I do.' His sense of control was returning and the words sounded sharp.

'But isn't that…?' She paused, her eyes meeting his, and he said nothing, hoping she wouldn't echo his thoughts. 'A bit too intimate?'

'It's New Year's Eve, Natalie.' He liked the way it felt to say her full name and revelled in the spark of annoyance that leapt to life in her eyes. 'We are alone in this house. It would be churlish to do any different.'

'Maybe we should try and get back to London before it's too late?' She glanced out at the falling snow.

'It is already too late. I have checked online. Travel isn't advisable. This snow has caught the forecaster unawares and already many of the local roads here are not passable unless you are in a four-wheel drive.' He didn't particularly relish the idea of being snowed in with a woman who made him want things he had no right to, but fate had dealt them this hand and he was adamant he wasn't going to succumb to the temptation that was Natalie Rogers. Not while she was working for him.

'Thank goodness I have a booking at a local bed and breakfast tonight,' she said light-heartedly, and shrugged her shoulders, moving past him, her arm brushing against his. A strange sensation zipped around him, startling him.

'I don't think even that will be possible.'

'I can't stay here. Alone with you. All night.' The horror at such a suggestion rang clear in her voice.

'We will dine together, so make any necessary changes you need to. There is no reason to be hiding out here all night.' As soon as he'd spoken he knew they had been the wrong words.

'Hiding? Why would I be hiding?' A hint of mockery was veiled beneath the amusement in her eyes and he couldn't do anything else other than look into them.

'You've already made it perfectly clear that spending time with me isn't what you want to do.' He quirked a brow at her, unable to resist building on the flirtatious mood as it swirled around them, intensifying by the second.

'It isn't professional.'

'I think we can dispense with such professionalism—just for this evening, don't you? It is New Year's Eve and due to circumstances beyond our control we will be here alone all night.' She was setting very clear boundaries, something he would normally adhere to, but they only urged him on, pushing him to take up the challenge her body was unconsciously sending to his.

'I can't stay here. Not all night,' Tilly gasped out, incredulity in every word as the reality of the situation hit her. 'I have to be at Vanessa's house tomorrow. It's her engagement party on New Year's Day.'

She knew she was rambling and blushing

again and it infuriated her. She always did it when she was anxious or nervous. When she looked at Xavier the smile tilting his lips upwards served only to panic her further, as did the flutter of awareness growing inside her.

'I'm very sorry, *cara*, but you won't be going anywhere tonight. It's just you and me.' The sexy undercurrent in his voice was clear, but if he thought he was going to take advantage of the situation he was very much mistaken. She wasn't going to fall into a heap at his feet, bowled over by his sexy accent and good looks. She would not be added to his list of conquests.

'No,' she said, not liking the way he made her so flustered as once again his fingers brushed over hers. 'I have somewhere to stay.'

Staying here wasn't going to be very professional—anything but, in fact. It was bad enough she had to give in to his insistence that she join him at the table for the New Year's Eve dinner, but staying all night wouldn't do her reputation any good at all.

'Assuming, of course, you could actually leave here.' He sounded far too self-assured and it crossed her mind that he might have engineered this.

As soon as the thought came she squashed

it. She was fooling herself with such notions. A man like Xavier Moretti wouldn't engineer time with *her*. She hadn't seen anything of life, as Jason had boldly told her. She was just a naïve inexperienced twenty-three-year-old who was in danger of reading too much into Xavier's flirtation.

'No, I have to be at Vanessa's party. I can't let her down.' Desperation sounded in her voice. Being at Vanessa's party was a lot more than just attending a party. It was proving, to herself and her friend, that she'd moved on from last year.

'Did you not just say the party was tomorrow?'

She frowned at him, unable to settle her nerves, unsure if she was more frightened of driving in such conditions or staying here alone with him. 'Yes, tomorrow evening.'

'Then call and explain. You can leave tomorrow if the weather permits. In the meantime, I suggest you bring in your luggage and I will show you to your room.'

'My room?' Everything was spiralling out of control and she didn't like it one bit. She constantly strove to be in control as much as possible. Control was the mainstay of her life.

'But of course. I was expecting guests and

have rooms made up.' He smiled at her, his dark eyes sparking with mischief. He was enjoying this, damn him.

Resigned to the fact she had little choice, she sighed her discontent and took her van keys from the table. 'Very well, I'll fetch my things.'

'*Bene.* Don't forget your party dress.'

She whirled round to face him. 'What?'

'Your party dress, the one you planned to wear at your friend's party. You will need it tonight.' Each word was so deep and sultry it was far too sexy and she couldn't think straight. Why on earth was he talking about party dresses?

'Why?'

'Because it's New Year's Eve and we will dine together in style.'

CHAPTER THREE

XAVIER TOOK TILLY'S small overnight bag from her, trying not to notice the ever-present sizzle whenever he got too close. 'I'll show you to your room.'

'There must be a way I can get to the bed and breakfast.' She looked at him, the determined jut of her chin showing just how much she didn't want to be alone here with him. 'I can't just stay here.'

He took a few steps away from her, giving himself badly needed distance. 'What kind of man do you think I am, to allow you to drive late at night in such treacherous driving conditions? I have a house full of rooms and not a single guest and will not allow it.'

'If you put it like that...' She looked at him, the warning in her eyes shining out at him. 'But only for tonight. Whatever happens, I have to leave for Vanessa's party tomorrow.'

'We are both at the mercy of the weather,

Natalie. This way.' He marched into the hall, past the Christmas tree and up the wide staircase. He knew she was following, every nerve in his body alerted to her proximity.

He paused briefly at the top of the stairs and looked down at her. She stopped and met his gaze. Tension zipped between them and he inhaled deeply, instilling control back into his body, trying to dull his heightened senses. It was as if her body was speaking to his, despite those barriers she'd erected.

He continued to the far end of the house, a view of the grounds, covered in snow, visible from the windows as they made their way along the corridor. It was the furthest room from his and, judging by the way she made him feel, that was a good thing. He hadn't ever been tested like this and he'd forgotten what temptation was. The accident had changed him, made him immune. Evidently, that wasn't the case any more.

He opened the door of the bedroom at the end of the corridor and went in, placed her bag at the foot of the bed and watched Tilly as she came in. She moved around the room, her pleasure in its opulence showing in her innocent delight at her surroundings.

'Are you sure I should be staying here?' she

asked tentatively, as she looked up at the four-poster bed, draped in cream and gold fabric. 'I'm not strictly a guest.'

'I invited you to join me for dinner this evening, so now you are a guest.' His tone was abrupt as he fought the emotions she stirred in him. She glanced at him, questions and anxiety filling her beautiful blue eyes.

'Not in the true sense,' she said softly, and moved towards the windows and the ever-darkening view of the grounds. 'It's snowing even more heavily now.'

As far as he was concerned, it could snow for days. Nothing was more appealing than the thought of finding out more about Natalie Rogers. He wanted to break down her barriers of professionalism and disciplined organisation to discover the passionate woman behind them, because he knew such a woman existed within her. Intuitively he sensed she was different from any woman he'd ever dated. She had an earthly innocence about her and was totally unaware of just how alluring she was.

'I will leave you to unpack.' He had to go now, before he pulled her into his arms, because if he did, she wouldn't be slipping away from him as easily as she had done earlier.

* * *

For the rest of the afternoon Tilly had worked hard, changing the menu once more and setting the table in the grand dining room. Anything other than think of the man she was effectively trapped here with. She should feel worried, scared even. She hardly knew him, but there was something between them, as if they did know one another and whatever it was she was determined to ignore it.

It was dark now but she could still see the large flakes of snow falling past the window, dashing any last hopes she'd had of leaving later this evening for the bed and breakfast as planned.

She and Xavier were snowed in. It was so different from last year's debacle and not at all what she needed. This New Year's Eve she would be in the company of a man who set her pulse racing with just one dark and brooding glance, something Jason had never done.

From the hallway she heard the tall elegant grandfather clock strike seven and knew she couldn't put it off any longer. It was time to change into the dress she planned to wear at Vanessa's engagement party—if she ever got there.

The choice of an elegant black dress that

oozed glamour and sex appeal had seemed perfect as she'd tried it on in the shop. It would prove to everyone that she'd moved on, grown up even. Now, with its plunging back, it was completely inappropriate but, then, so was staying in jeans and a jumper or even her uniform. She was worried what Xavier would think. It was too much for their impromptu meal together, but it was all she had.

Maybe Xavier wouldn't have changed. The thought gave her hope as she crossed the hallway, glancing distractedly at the Christmas tree and wondering who had opened presents from beneath its decorated branches just a few days ago. She paused on the bottom step and reached out to touch a sparkling gold decoration, her fingers sending it spinning, the light catching it.

She longed for the day she could create the perfect Christmas for a family of her own, but her childhood had made it difficult to allow love into her life. With a sigh, she knew she might never have a family of her own. She'd loved Jason, he had been her best friend, but he'd dumped her, not even caring it had been their wedding day.

Christmas this year should have been their first as a married couple, but instead it had been very quiet, which was for the best. Just as taking this contract to get away from London had been. She'd been so excited when the email had arrived, stating how highly recommended her business was. It was just the boost the business needed.

Movement at the top of the stairs caught her attention and she glanced up, instantly wishing she hadn't. Xavier stood there, watching her moment of reflection. He was dressed in a full evening suit that all but clung to his body, accentuating his height and the broad width of his shoulders. The image he created was one of perfection, straight out of a movie.

He was devastatingly handsome. Just seeing him like this did untold things to her heart rate, setting off a ripple of flutters inside her stomach. A dart of panic rushed through her, quashing those inappropriate thoughts. She was going to have to spend the evening with this man and engage in conversation in a setting that was far too intimate. What had she got herself into?

He began to descend the stairs, his gaze locking with hers, and once again that movie moment made her feel light-headed. His lithe yet powerful movements were something she'd never seen in a man other than on the big screen. Had she slipped from the real world the moment she'd crossed the threshold of Wimble Manor?

'Buona sera,' he said, as he stopped on the same stair she was currently rooted to, his dark eyes full of knowing amusement. A little spike of anger darted through her. He knew full well he created an image women craved and right now was exploiting it to its full potential. Well, it wasn't going to work on her.

'I'm just going to change.' The throaty whisper that came from her sent a blush to her cheeks and she resisted the urge to flee and run upstairs as fast as she could. Instead she smiled at him in the most professional way possible.

'I'll wait for you in the lounge.' His sensual accent stirred new sensations deep within her, but outwardly she remained composed. She had to. To show him anything else would be a mistake.

'I will be as quick as I can,' she said lightly, and began to walk calmly up the stairs, while inside she fought the urge to bolt like a startled animal.

'Take your time, Natalie.'

She closed her eyes as she heard her name spoken so beautifully. She knew he was still watching her. Her skin tingled from his intense gaze and with every step she took it became harder to ignore, but she wouldn't give him the satisfaction of turning around yet. As she reached the top of the stairs and looked down at him, their positions reversed, her heart hammered so loudly it almost echoed around the old walls of the manor.

She wanted to give him a curt reply, show him his charm didn't work with her, but her ability to speak had deserted her.

He smiled, his brows lifting suggestively, and the full force of his power washed over her. 'We have all night, no?'

She blinked at the deeper meaning in those seductively accented words. If he thought she would just fall meekly into the role of his new conquest, simply because she was the only woman available, he was very much mistaken. 'I will join you when I'm ready.'

With that she flounced away, his soft and incredibly sexy laugh following her along the corridor. This wasn't what she'd planned for New Year's Eve. After Jason had abandoned her, she'd wanted nothing more from this New Year's Eve than to hide behind her new business and away from friends who thought they knew just what she needed.

She walked into her room, flicked on the lamps and drew the heavy curtains against the cold night and turned her attention to her dress. How could she wear that tonight? In the company of a man—her client—who made her feel and think things she had no right to? He was dangerous. She had no idea why, no reasons to justify it. But she sensed it.

Was she reading more into their exchanges, allowing her head to be turned by his charm? Was her judgement coloured by the almost undeniable attraction she felt for him? He'd only flirted mildly with her and she knew a man like him, who had his pick of high-flying beauties, wouldn't be interested in her. Not only was she a jilted bride but she was a virgin, far too inexperienced.

She may be supressing the attraction which had simmered to life since the moment she'd arrived here, but he was being the playboy he was reputed to be.

'You'll do well to remember that, Tilly Rogers,' she said to her reflection, as she looked at the gorgeous black silk dress that had transformed her from hired staff to dinner guest.

She thought of Xavier in the tailored suit that had instantly increased that sizzle of attraction for him. Would he feel the same when he saw her in this dress? Would he think she was attractive? Would he want her? She smiled at the notion of him falling for her as if they were playing out their own fairy-tale.

Annoyed at the direction her thoughts had taken, she twisted her hair into something that resembled a chignon, wishing she'd brought her tried and tested smart black dress instead of this extravagant number that had no place in her life. She didn't know what she'd been thinking when she'd bought it. Glamour and sophistication weren't in her genetic make-up.

She fastened the straps of her sandals, also part of her impulse buy, and with once last check in the mirror left her room. The walk back downstairs became more infused with anticipation each step she took.

What was the matter with her? She wasn't going on a date. He wasn't even her bucket list romantic fling. She was only joining him for dinner because the situation with the weather had left them alone here on New Year's Eve.

What could be so wrong about that?

As she paused at the bottom of the stairs, absently taking in the Christmas tree, she had the strangest notion that going into the room where Xavier waited and spending the evening with him would change everything. How could a snowstorm and a dinner do that?

Primal stirrings of longing rushed through Xavier as he waited for Tilly—or Natalie, as he'd come to think of her. He enjoyed using her full name. But it was more than that. Something had burst to life between them since the moment he'd first seen her, standing in the snowy courtyard. Whatever that was, it had drawn him, lured him with the promise of things he wanted but knew he couldn't have, and not just because she was hiding behind her job. He didn't deserve such things.

He took a deep steadying breath and looked into the flames of the log fire he'd lit before changing. Natalie was different. She was the kind of woman who made a man instinctively want to offer protection. She evoked a need to cherish and love.

As that last thought drifted unbidden through his mind the door opened and she walked in, her cool demeanour so sophisticated he couldn't believe she was the same bubbly person who'd arrived this morning. She looked absolutely stunning. The black silk of her dress caressed every curve of her body, but she was swathed in an aura that made her almost untouchable. Was that her defence against the attraction he knew she too felt?

'Cosi bella.' The Italian compliment left his lips before he'd realised he'd spoken, but it was the truth. She was beautiful.

The black silk of her dress emphasised her stunning figure and his gaze lingered on her bare shoulders, imagining what it would be like to press his lips against the creamy softness of her skin. She blushed beneath his scrutiny and looked away, confirming his suspicion of defensive barriers against the steadily growing attraction.

'The fire looks inviting.' She was obviously intent on taking his attention away from her and maybe that was for the best, but a hint of huskiness lingered in her voice, belying the composure she displayed. 'I've always loved the idea of a real fire.'

'Have you never spent an evening in front of the warmth of the flames with someone special?' He reached for the bottle of champagne he'd put to cool and hoped the cold liquid would douse the heat burning within him as the image of the two of them doing just that came unbidden to his mind.

He popped the cork and she gave a startled little gasp, her eyes meeting his as she blushed.

'No, I haven't. Unless you count being in country pubs with friends.'

He handed her a flute of champagne, trying to beat down the irrational jealousy that filled him, thinking of her sitting in a cosy pub with another man. 'And now you are forced to endure my company for the evening.'

'Endure is a bit strong,' she said quickly, as her slender fingers held the stem of the flute, her gaze meeting his boldly. 'Enjoy is a far better word.'

He chinked his flute against hers. '*Salute!* To enjoyment.'

'To enjoyment,' she echoed his toast, a small and incredibly sexy smile playing about her lips. 'And I'm sorry your plans for this evening, have gone wrong.'

'I very much like the alternative.' He raised his glass slightly in a silent toast to those changed plans. Her eyes darted from his, breaking the contact.

She laughed. A soft, seductive laugh that didn't diffuse the tension, as he suspected she'd wanted it to. Instead it grew stronger, more intense. She moved away from him, away from the cream stone fireplace that must have seen many such moments over the generations.

'You might want to reserve judgement, or

even call off the whole evening. You wouldn't
be the first to do that.' With the light-hearted
warning lingering in the air, Tilly put down her
flute of champagne and now that distance between them had been reinstated seemed content to make eye contact. 'If you will excuse me
for a moment, I will organise the first course.'

His first instinct was to offer to help, but
after the potent exchange, loaded with pent-
up passion, he needed space. If he closed his
eyes, even for just a moment, he could imagine all this was real, that they were here out
of choice. That not only did she want to spend
the night in his bed, that he wouldn't have to
worry about the scars that had made casual
nights of passion impossible since the accident.

He snapped his eyes open. Imagining such
things was impossible. They could never be
anything to each other—not yet at least.

Tilly returned to the lounge to see Xavier
standing rigidly before the fire, his face a stern
mask of irritation. Was that because he'd forgotten himself just now and flirted with her?
Did he already regret offering to celebrate New
Year's Eve together?

'Would you like to come through to the dining room?' She injected as much professional-

ism as she could into those words, reminding herself that, no matter what had happened between them just now, she was still working—for him.

'*Bene.*' The word was a soft growl, an almost feral sound and his expression one of agitation, as he crossed the room.

She turned and walked towards the dining room, forgetting the daringly low cut of the back of her dress as she cursed the heels she'd once thought would be fun to wear. Now she knew her walk was slow and hoped he didn't think she was flaunting herself in front of him. She couldn't get to her chair fast enough.

'Allow me.' The hard tone of his voice spoke volumes about his annoyance at having to dine alone with her.

She must have imagined the undercurrent of sexual tension that had surrounded them after she'd arrived in the lounge. Maybe it was because she wanted this dark and dangerous attraction to him to become reality. As if putting on the dress, being here in this house with Xavier, was giving her a chance to be someone different, step away from her past and sample a world of complete fantasy for just one night.

A reckless thought raced through her mind about the romantic fling on her bucket list.

Could this be the night? When she proved to herself she'd moved on from her almost wedding day? Denial careered into that wayward thought, stopping it abruptly.

She sat on her chair as he stood behind it for a moment longer. A tingle skipped down her spine and it was all she could do not to arch her back as the sensation speared warmth through her. It was as if he'd touched her, trailed his fingers down over her bare skin.

'Thank you.' She forced out the words and sat back against the chair, trying to stop the way her heart raced, its thumping rhythm so loud he must hear it.

'Prego.'

Moments later Xavier sat opposite her at the festively decorated table. Candles glowed intimately and the pasta starter cooled as their gazes locked once more. What was happening to her? This new and overwhelming pull of attraction and heart-pounding desire was taking over.

He is your client. The words shouted inside her head.

'I apologise for changing the menu a second time.' Once she'd realised they would be eating alone she'd adapted the menu choices. Now she wished she hadn't. Time away from his dark

and powerful eyes was just what she needed—
if she was to retain her usual composure.

He held her gaze for a moment longer, not
saying a word, and she resisted the temptation
to bite her bottom lip, the way she always did
when she was anxious, in an attempt to stop
herself saying silly things. Under no circumstances did she want this man to know he made
her feel apprehensive. The air around them was
hot and heavy, throbbing with intensity, as he
finally began his food.

'*Delizioso.*' He nodded his approval and the
anxiety that had been building in her all day
began to slip away, enabling her to eat something at least.

As he finished his starter he sat back and
looked at her, increasing her pulse rate again.
'So tell me, Natalie. What is it you are hiding
from this New Year's Eve?'

The unexpected question nearly made her
choke, but thankfully she managed to avoid
that spectacle and met his gaze boldly, annoyed
to see his brows lift, prompting her for an answer. She reached for her glass of wine and took
a sip as expectancy stretched between them.

'What makes you think I'm hiding from
anything?' She didn't like the nervous wobble in her words. 'I'm here, working.'

'A beautiful woman like you shouldn't be alone on New Year's Eve and definitely not working. I can't believe you do not have at least one admirer who wants to share this evening with you.' His deliciously accented words made her stomach flutter and for one crazy moment she imagined he was that admirer, that he wanted to be with her, instead of being forced into her company.

'I wanted to work tonight.' Her matter-of-fact words came so fluidly it was as if she'd rehearsed them. She'd used that excuse again and again in recent weeks as the party invitations had arrived. There was just one person who'd seen through it. Vanessa.

He smiled, one of satisfaction, but it still made him look deliciously handsome. 'You are hiding, then.'

What would he say if he knew the truth? Would it kill whatever hummed between them? She certainly hoped so, because she was finding it ever more difficult not to notice the way her body felt each time he looked at her.

'Not exactly. My fiancé called off our wedding exactly a year ago today.' The sharp words hurtled out. Just bringing Jason into her mind cooled the effect Xavier was having on her.

He sat back in his chair, his fingers slowly turning the stem of the wine glass. 'So you thought that working this year was preferable to partying?'

'Something like that.' She wished she hadn't begun this conversation. In a bid to quell the tension, which was loaded with passion, she'd already said too much. 'I'll get the next course.'

Before he could say anything else she left the room, as gracefully and quickly as her heels allowed. In the kitchen she dished up the venison casserole and croquette potatoes that the wintery weather had inspired and forced down the pain of Jason's betrayal.

Footsteps alerted her to Xavier's presence and she pretended to be busy with the food, not wanting to look at him and see the same pity on his face that her friends and family bestowed on her. Pity she didn't deserve, not when ultimately it had been her fault the wedding hadn't happened. She'd just followed through from being school friends to fulfilling everyone's expectations of marriage. Jason had been the only constant in her life, but for him, at least, it hadn't been enough.

She heard Xavier put down the starter plates, but couldn't acknowledge him yet, keeping resolutely turned away. He stopped directly behind her and her breathing deepened as her almost bare back tingled from his nearness and she vehemently wished she hadn't changed out of her jeans and jumper.

'Can I offer help?' The husky note of his voice, to her dismay, made her shiver visibly. 'You are cold.'

'A little,' she lied, as she turned to face him, alarmed at how close he was. 'You hired me to cater for this dinner party and should not be helping.'

She picked up the hot dish of the main course with her waitressing cloth and left the kitchen, desperate to get away from the heat he'd surrounded her with. But if she'd thought things would be easier as they sat at the table again, she had been wrong. Their polite exchanges were merely a smokescreen for something much bigger.

'Your fiancé, he was a fool.' Xavier finished his meal and placed his napkin on the table, intently watching every move she made.

'You can't say that. You don't know anything about him.' Instinctively she protected Jason. It hadn't been entirely Jason's fault. He'd only been reacting to her inability to show him love. When her father had died her mother had sought solace with a new man and she had felt abandoned. All she'd wanted had been to feel special and Jason had done that, first as a friend, then as her boyfriend, but never as her lover.

'That may be so, but I do know he was a fool to let a woman like you go.' A light smile lifted his lips and she found herself wondering what it would be like to be kissed by him. Instantly she dismissed the thought as totally unprofessional. It was so unlike her and guilt filled her for thinking it when the only man she'd kissed was Jason.

Again that item on her bucket list nudged to the forefront of her mind. It was so out of character for her that Vanessa had been shocked when she'd told her, but hadn't let her forget the idea, adamant it was *just* what she needed. She'd reminded her of it earlier when she'd called her to say she was snowed in at the manor. Could this really be her chance to tick that off her list, to prove to herself she was over Jason, without getting her heart broken?

No. She was here professionally and wouldn't jeopardise her business reputation for one night of excitement, however tempting Xavier might be.

Xavier sensed there was a lot more she wasn't telling him. To be defending her ex-fiancé so strongly, she must still love him. But why love someone who'd hurt you, walking out on you when it had most counted?

He done exactly that to his long-term girl-friend when she'd left him literally hanging in the hospital, too disgusted to even sit with him. Carlotta had taken it so well he'd seriously questioned if she'd ever loved him and was relieved he'd resisted prompts from her and his family, before the accident, to make that final and permanent commitment. At least he hadn't had to deal with a divorce as well as the knowledge he'd destroyed Paulo's family.

Tilly stood up abruptly, dragging his thoughts back from those dark days, effectively ending the conversation. 'Dessert?'

The husky tone of her voice pulled his thoughts back from those painful months after the accident. Painful not because Carlotta had shown her true shallow nature but because of the guilt that racked him every time he thought of the accident and the devastation it had caused.

He let his gaze travel down Tilly's slender body, allowing her gorgeous figure to ground him and pull him back from that abyss. On her beautiful face was an expression of hesitancy, mixed with the composure she'd been fighting to retain all night.

A stab of hot lust shot through him. It wasn't just the challenge she'd set before him, it was much more—and almost impossible to ignore.

He wanted her—more than he'd wanted any woman.

'Let's abandon this formality.' The need to break out, to rebel against what was right, surged through him.

'What do you mean?' The shock in her voice was clear, her blue eyes wide with disbelief.

'The fire in the lounge is so much more inviting, no?'

'Yes, it is.' She lowered her lashes, blocking him out, but even so her body called to his, beckoned him with the lure of desire.

'Bene.' He got up and moved around the table towards her. She met his gaze again, her gorgeous eyes wide and luminous, and he felt something squeeze tight around his chest. It had been a long time since a woman had affected him so potently.

Suddenly she moved away from him and began clearing the table. 'I will see to this first.' The matter-of-fact words cooled his ardour, reminding him she was not the kind of woman to have affairs, the kind who wanted just what at the moment he could offer. He had to remember he'd hired her for this evening's dinner party, which in itself was an added complication.

Before he had time to process those thoughts properly she left the room, carrying things back to the kitchen. He picked up other items from the table and strode through to the kitchen where the bright lights subdued what had arced between them—and highlighted reality.

'I have a few things to do then I will bring dessert through to the lounge.' She turned and looked at him, the wariness in her eyes halting him in his tracks. She was warning him without words to keep away, telling him she didn't want to pursue the attraction, and after what she'd just told him he'd be heartless to force her. She was still in love with another man, even though her body called to his. But ignoring her was proving difficult.

'Allow me to help.'

'No.' The shock in that word startled him, and he looked at her in question. 'No, thank you. This is my job, Signor Moretti, I'm not here to be wined and dined. I'm paid to be here—working.'

She was either putting them both firmly in their places or laying down an even bigger challenge. His pulse leapt at the thought, but he knew, deep down, it wasn't that. She was right. Her brief story about last New Year's Eve only confirmed she wanted more than a night of passion and an expensive parting gift. She wasn't the kind of woman who sought such nights, she never would be. He couldn't give a woman like Tilly what she wanted.

'Very well,' he said firmly. 'But I expect you to join me in the lounge. I have no intention of welcoming in the New Year alone.'

'But…' She searched for more excuses.

'You will join me,' he said sternly, and she looked up at him and the expression on her face soothed his ruffled demeanour. She looked vulnerable and so very beautiful. 'For just one glass of champagne. To toast in the New Year.'

CHAPTER FOUR

Tilly's heart rate had barely slowed after Xavier had left the kitchen. Unable to do anything for a while, she had just stood looking out of the window, watching the large snowflakes drift past, so white against the darkness of the night.

For the last hour she'd kept reminding herself she was working for Signor Moretti, as she tried hard to think of him. Anything to stay on a professional level, because talking about Jason and last New Year's Eve with him had allowed things to slip into something more intimate.

After what had just happened, her body hummed spectacularly with desire, in a way she'd never known, one unacceptable in every way. She'd tried to avoid spending further time with him, not liking his probing questions about last year. She had reminded him she was working for him, but it hadn't cooled the heat in his eyes. She was going to have to be on her guard. She had no intention of breaking her rules and certainly not of becoming just another woman to him.

She stood on the threshold of the lounge, not daring to push open the door and walk in, sensing that doing so would change her—for ever. The clock in the hall struck the half-hour. Half past eleven. Very soon it would be midnight and her contract would end. She should be leaving, but fate had other ideas and she wasn't sure she could hide behind her mask of professionalism—or that she even wanted to.

As the chimes fell silent she pushed open the dark wooden door, feeling the warmth of the fire meet her. Her hands were shaking and she paused, looking at Xavier, the sense that everything would be different after tonight becoming greater.

'Infine.' The soft Italian word and the hint of amusement in it caressed her senses as she walked into the room, trying to leave her insecurities outside. She didn't want him to know just how these last few hours had already affected her.

The image of Xavier standing close to the open fire, his tall and toned body commanding her attention, was almost too much. The formal black suit only added to his sex appeal and she made an effort to drag her gaze from him. She had to stop looking at him so wantonly. She looked instead at the many paintings hanging around the room, but that didn't stop her wondering what it would be like to be held in his arms or kissed by his lips. She seriously doubted if anything could, now the sizzle of attraction filled the very air she breathed.

'Yes, finally,' she translated with a smile, inwardly berating herself. She needed to do something to remind both of them exactly what her position here tonight was. Hired help. 'Sorry to have kept you waiting, but I had some work to do.'

'Come.' He gestured to the sofa in front of the fire, a smile playing about his lips suggesting he knew she'd been hiding in the kitchen. Or was that her guilty conscience for having done exactly that? 'It is almost midnight. Join me for a glass of champagne.'

His dark eyes sparked with something she didn't want to recognise as she walked to the sofa and sat demurely in front of the fire, the soft warmth of the fabric offering some protection from his devouring looks. She took the glass of champagne he handed her, knowing she shouldn't drink any more after the wine she'd enjoyed with the meal.

With devilment lingering in his smile, he resumed his position by the fire and raised his glass to her, then sipped at the bubbly liquid. She did the same, tasting the delicious golden bubbles, enjoying the sensation of being spoilt.

'This is not what I had expected for this evening,' she said as she held her glass, determined not to indulge in too much of this luxury, or get carried away by it. 'I don't suppose it was for you either. I'm sorry your family couldn't get here, that you have to make do with me.'

'That is not such a hardship.' His deep and accented voice tempted her to look directly into those dark, mesmerising eyes. 'I am pleased you are here. It would have been a very quiet New Year all alone.'

His gentle laugh, so seductive, unleashed a tremor of pleasure through her. He was making it sound as if he genuinely wanted to be here with her tonight. That he wasn't at all put out he would be sharing his New Year celebrations with his caterer.

She took a sip of champagne, trying to remember he was a playboy with a big reputation and she was very different from the kind of women he dated. She didn't have a sophisticated bone in her body. She was just being fanciful, filling her head with romantic notions that had no hope of fulfilment.

What she should be doing was relaxing and enjoying the evening for what it was—a brief interlude in her life. The chance to sample a lifestyle she only saw from the other side, one night in a world of complete fantasy with this sexy Italian, a world where Tilly Rogers didn't exist, just Natalie.

The temptation to fulfil the romantic fling she'd added to her bucket list intensified. Hastily she pushed that thought aside. If she did have that fling, it wouldn't be with a man who had no other choice but her. It would have to be with a man who truly desired her—for that night at least.

'I appreciate your invitation,' she said, boldly holding his gaze, trying not to read too much into the intensity there. 'It's a change to be able to sit and enjoy the food and wine— and wear this.'

She'd added a touch of humour, trying to lighten the mood, but judging by the smouldering look in his eyes had failed completely. All she'd done had been to draw his attention to her.

'You look very beautiful this evening.' His words were soft and caressing, but she didn't miss the fierceness deep within them. *'Molto bella.'*

She looked away into the orange flicker of the flames, feeling herself blush again. Did he have to keep slipping into delicious and seductive Italian? 'Thank you, but I don't think the lady in your life would be very impressed to hear you say that.'

To her surprise he laughed and she looked at him again, irritated to be the focus of his amusement. He walked to a small table, picked the champagne bottle from its bucket of iced water, refilled both crystal flutes and then sat at the other end of the sofa.

'There isn't a woman in my life.'

'But I thought…' she began, then stopped. Images she'd seen on the internet of the beautiful brunette who'd accompanied him to a party were still clear in her mind. Then she remembered his reputation. He was not a man to settle down.

He stretched out his long legs and relaxed back into the corner of the sofa, one arm draped along the back, his hand unnervingly close to her. 'You thought I was in a relationship?'

'Well, yes, actually I did.' She couldn't keep

the flustered tone from her voice, unable to decide if it was the topic of conversation or the fact that she could feel her bare back burning because his hand was close as it rested on the cushions behind her. And his legs, long and strong, stretched out towards her, all but trapping her.

'After ending a long-term relationship, I prefer to remain uncommitted.' His message was clear. He only looked for brief affairs, just as his reputation had suggested. Even more reason not to get charmed into something she would regret.

'I see,' she said quietly, and looked down into her glass, watching the bubbles rising to the surface then disappearing, wondering if she really would regret a kiss from this man.

His sudden movement as he leant forward nearly made her spill her champagne and she drew in a sharp breath, but as her eyes met with the darkness in his, her pulse leapt. 'I'm sure that after last year you feel the same too.'

'If by that you mean I have had a string of meaningless love affairs, you are very much mistaken. I am not that sort of woman.' Indignation rushed over her as words of defence hurtled from her. What would his reaction be if she told him she was a virgin?

Confusion muddled her as her earlier thoughts of having a fling with him burned shamelessly in her mind. She wanted to jump up, leave the room, but something kept her there. Something she didn't want to accept kept her there with Xavier, sharing a moment she knew would never have happened if events hadn't conspired against them, cutting them off from the real world.

'I know,' he said softly, his increasingly black eyes looking into hers, sending shivers of pleasure down her spine. 'That is why I didn't give in to the temptation to kiss you, even though you wanted me to.'

'You arrogant...' The contents of her flute spilt onto her dress as she jumped up to get away from this self-assured man, unbalancing in an attempt to avoid his legs. Instinctively she reached out to save herself, only to find his arms around her, pulling her against the firmness of his body as he leapt to his feet.

'You were saying?' The humour in his voice fuelled the furious fire that raged inside her. It wasn't just fury at his assumption that he could have kissed her, it was anger at herself. He must have known, as they'd stood looking out at the snowy landscape this morning, that she'd wanted him to kiss her.

She glared up at him, her breathing deep and hard as he held her against him, the thin silk of her dress little protection from the heat of his body. She could feel the strength of his arms as they held her. Her heart thumped so hard she was sure he'd not only hear it but feel it too.

'Your charm and flirtatious manner might work with other women, but it will not work with me.' She should push him away, prove the point, but she couldn't. Her body was acting against her mind, seeking what it wanted, not what was best.

'Because you are still in love with the man you should have married?' His eyes narrowed as he frowned, but the spark of desire within them couldn't be concealed.

'Yes,' she lied. Surely he'd let her go if he thought that. It was the best form of defence, even though now she'd finally realised what she and Jason had shared had been friendship, not love. 'And because I am here as your caterer, not your latest conquest.'

'I don't believe you.' Xavier looked into Tilly's blue eyes, seeing them swirl with desire, echoing the hum within his body. Was that possible if she was still in love with another man? Wouldn't she have pushed him away? She certainly wouldn't look so sexy and kissable, her lips parting in invitation as she held his gaze. If her heart loved another man her eyes would be blazing with indignation, not desire.

'Well, it's true,' she said firmly, finally pushing against him.

He let her go, resisting the temptation to taste those full lips, but her eyes looked so full of desire, so brimming with passion yet to be tasted, it was almost impossible. She was right about being his hired help and he'd respect that—for now.

She bent and brushed her hand over the champagne mark on her dress and he knew it was to avoid looking at him, preventing him seeing what had been shining from her eyes. She couldn't hide that raw passion and desire. It was too late.

'Then why are you here tonight? Why aren't you with this Jason, telling him how much you love him?' he taunted mercilessly. He couldn't help himself. Natalie Rogers was doing untold things to him, forcing a new emotion that felt very much like jealousy to the fore.

She stood up straight, the worry of her dress abandoned, but her irritation with him clearly not. 'Need I remind you again? I'm here, working —for you.'

The feisty tone of her voice brought a smile to his face, which, to his amusement, antagonised her further. 'More champagne? You cannot toast in the New Year with an empty glass. Midnight is minutes away—as is the end of your contract.'

For a moment he thought she was going to refuse. Her eyes sparked with passion-induced anger and he wanted her more than he'd wanted any woman. The black silk of her dress seemed sculpted over her breasts, which rose and fell with each breath.

She was beautiful. Perfect.

She was also a reminder of all he didn't deserve to have.

'Just one more glass.' Her husky whisper pulled him back from those thoughts, from the need to punish and deprive himself of happiness or love. He didn't deserve either, not when one mistake—his mistake—had snatched Paulo's life and with it the happiness of an entire family.

'*Grazie,*' he said, his voice rough and rasping as he pushed the demons away, not wanting them tormenting him tonight. He poured the last of the champagne into each flute, feeling her gaze on him. What would she think of him if she knew the truth? Would the hot sizzle of desire she couldn't quite conceal still radiate from her? Or would she be like Carlotta? Cold and disgusted?

'Thank you.' She took the flute of champagne from him but couldn't meet his gaze, her long dark lashes lowering over her eyes, locking him out.

He strode over to the fire, placed his champagne on the mantelpiece and tossed another log onto the fire, stoking the flames, making them leap, matching the way his desire for her had burst into life from the thought of just one kiss.

'You must be regretting taking this contract.' He spoke firmly as he looked into the fire, its heat matching that which still pumped around his body.

'I took the job because I didn't want to be forced to party and celebrate—or remember.' Her voice was unwavering, the husky whisper of moments ago gone, replaced by total strength.

'He is a fool.' He growled the words out and turned to look at her. 'To throw away a woman like you.'

'It wasn't quite like that,' she said, and moved towards him, drawn by the warmth of the fire. The clock in the hall chimed, marking the last fifteen minutes of the year, and she looked up at him. 'We'd been together since school and I suppose we drifted into wedding plans, not wanting to disappoint our families. It was always expected we'd marry.'

The resigned tone of her voice, the acceptance of what she'd just said didn't fit with her earlier declarations of love for the man who'd left her. 'Yet you love him still?'

'Yes.' She looked down at her glass before taking a sip. 'He was my childhood sweetheart. I will always love him.'

'You should not waste your love on a man who walked away from you.' Involuntarily he took a step towards her, the connection between them strengthening. They both knew the pain of rejection, but it had been he who'd pushed Carlotta from his life after she'd all but rejected him.

'And do you speak from experience, Signor Moretti?'

The use of his surname shocked him momentarily, but he knew what she was trying to do. As the minutes ticked away the year and the spark of attraction increased, she wanted to instil propriety into the moment, remind him—and herself—of why they were here like this at all.

'I was involved in a racing accident that left me badly hurt and no longer the kind of company a glamorous model keeps. I couldn't offer Carlotta the luxurious lifestyle she craved any longer.' He wanted to tell her more, tell her he knew what it felt like to be rejected, but those words failed him. 'When I told her we were over she simply walked away and into the arms of another man.'

The soft gasp of shock that came from her lips made guilt rush through him and he turned away from her, looking again into the flames. He sensed her next to him before he felt her hand on his arm.

'I'm sorry,' she whispered softly.

What was she sorry for? His failed relationship, the accident, or forcing him to remember? 'It was for the best.' He snapped the words out, hoping to kill the conversation.

'When did it happen? The accident, I mean.' The tentative question nudged the memories back a little as her husky voice began to stir his desire again.

'Summer. Three years ago.' He looked into her eyes, saw the blue darken until they looked like a midnight sky. He was beginning to drown, pulled by an unknown force towards something he knew he shouldn't sample, let alone have.

'You sent her away because you were in hospital?' Incredulity poured from her, but he wondered what she would have done, faced with his rage and furious need to lash out. Would she have flinched, her face unable to hide her disgust when she saw his injuries for the first time? Would she have stayed around him as his mood had blackened and his guilt deepened?

'I was not the man she'd met, and couldn't offer the globetrotting life she sought. So I ended it.' The words sounded like a snarl as he slipped back in time, seeing again the moment that once lovely face had screwed up in selfish pity. '*Grazie a Dio!* It was for the best.'

'I don't know what to say.' The gentle concern in Tilly's eyes was almost too much. He was glad Carlotta had revealed her true self to him. It was just sad that it had taken such an accident to show him the kind of woman she was.

'When should you have married?' He needed to deflect attention from himself, prevent the horror of those months coming out into the open and infesting his dreams as they always did when he thought too much.

'An hour after Jason told me the engagement was off.'

* * *

Tilly clenched her teeth, biting back the tears. She couldn't let them fall now. Not here. Not in front of this man. She'd thought she was over Jason, over the way he'd called everything off so suddenly.

'*Dio mio.*'

The expletive was hotly followed by rapid Italian words she couldn't understand and her need to give to tears was swamped by the urge to laugh—in a way she hadn't done for months. How could she talk about it to Xavier and even find it funny? It was this place and being marooned from reality.

Exactly a year ago she should have married the man she'd believed to be her Mr Right. He'd been safe, comfortable, someone she'd grown up with, then he'd catapulted her into a new life, telling her she should live for the moment, as he'd done. Was that what she was fighting against now? A moment with an Italian playboy who set her pulse racing?

Xavier stepped close to her and reached out his hand, stroking the backs of his fingers across her cheek. The air cracked with tension as she continued to resist giving in to the temptation of a kiss. Seconds slowed to minutes as he moved closer still. So close she could smell his fresh masculine scent, taste it on her tongue.

She ached to be kissed by him, to feel his lips against hers.

From the hallway the old grandfather clock sounded the first strike of midnight. It chimed through the charged air and the small clock on the mantelpiece echoed it, ending the year and her contract.

'Midnight,' she whispered softly, unable to do anything else, the atmosphere was so laden and intense. His gaze fell to her lips and every breath she dragged in seemed to burn.

The chimes continued, showing out the old year and ringing in the new. Everything became hazy, except Xavier's handsome face. Had the world stopped turning?

'Buon Anno Nuovo.' His sensually deep voice sent ripples of tingling awareness all over her.

'Happy New Year.' Her soft barely-there whisper was almost drowned out by the thudding of her heart and the last stroke of midnight. She had to go right now. She wasn't ready for this. Before he could do anything to stop her, she left the room, carelessly putting her glass down as she passed a table.

'Natalie.'

He called after her, but she didn't stop until she was next to the Christmas tree he'd wanted banished from the house. Then she sensed him behind her and turned.

'Don't run from me, Natalie, not tonight.'

She looked at him, unable to decide if the undercurrent of vulnerability she heard in his voice was real. 'I have to go.'

'Stay.'

Was she really afraid to celebrate the New Year with a kiss or was she running because she wanted to be kissed? Would she regret it if she left now? Her heart thudded harder than ever as she looked at him. Her mouth felt dry, as if not a single drop of champagne had passed her lips.

'No. I can't.'

He didn't say anything but moved towards her, the intensity of moments ago still surrounding them. She couldn't take her eyes from his face and could hardly breathe as he moved closer.

His fingers brushed her cheek briefly before sliding into her thick hair and holding her firmly. Slowly he lowered his head, stopping before she could feel his lips on hers, and she looked into his eyes. Fireworks of passion exploded in them and beyond that display she saw something that made her want him more.

'Happy New Year, Natalie.' The deep tones of his voice sent sparks of heat around her body.

She swallowed hard, almost unable to form a single word as she responded instinctively in Italian. '*Buon Anno Nuovo*, Xavier.'

What was she doing? As his lips almost touched hers, she pulled back, but his hand in her hair held her. 'Your contract is over, Natalie, and you can't deny there is something between us tonight.'

Was he giving her permission to kiss him, to give in to the desire that thudded in her veins? His lips met hers, brushing so tenderly over them that a soft sigh escaped her. The kiss became harder, more demanding and she couldn't help herself.

She fought hard to keep her eyes open but it was all she could do to stop her lashes lowering. His lips tasted hers and she resisted the temptation to press herself against him, hot need rushing through her. This was just a New Year's kiss. Nothing more.

His fingers curled tightly in her hair, keeping her lips just where she really wanted them—beneath his. A small sigh of pleasure sounded in her throat as the kiss intensified, his tongue seeking hers.

She gave herself up to the ecstasy of the moment, her body filled with fiery heat. How could a kiss be so unbelievably hot? His lips trailed down her throat and her whole body trembled. He kissed her bare shoulders as he cupped her breast, the pad of his thumb grazing over her peaked nipple, causing her to drag in a breath of pure pleasure.

He moved against her and through the silk of her dress she could feel the firmness of his body, from the muscular chest to his strong thighs. Unashamedly she moulded herself against him, the hardness of his arousal pressing against her, tormenting her.

As passion threatened to overpower her, take away her last remnants of sanity, he pushed her away. Shock stunned her, freezing her mind and body. All she could hear was the thud of her pulse as her heart raced, but when she looked at him, the expression on his face had turned cold.

What had she done? What had she been thinking? Kissing Xavier Moretti like that?

The fierce look on his face left her in no doubt she'd gone too far, read too much into the flirtatious mood of the evening.

'That shouldn't have happened.' The husky tone of her voice cracked with raw desire that even she could hear. He continued to watch her, displeasure increasingly more evident in his eyes and the firm line of the lips that had just sent her senses into overdrive.

The temptation to turn and run upstairs was immense, but she must never let him know what his kiss had done. The world had stopped turning; everything except him had ceased to exist.

She stepped back, feeling a chill on her skin after the heat of being in front of the fire. Or was it the heat of his kiss? Those dark and wickedly brooding eyes didn't leave her face for one second, causing her cheeks to glow as a blush crept over them.

'Goodnight.' Thankfully firmness brushed aside the husky voice she'd just heard coming from herself. She stepped back again and the further she moved from him the more humiliation rose within her.

'*Buona notte*, Natalie.'

Damn him, he wasn't making this easy for her. He could at least say sorry. *But you kissed him back.* The traitorous voice in her head mocked her embarrassment and she dragged in a deep breath.

She had to get out of there. Slowly she turned to walk up the stairs, feeling him watching every move she made so intently she could hardly walk. After what seemed like an eternity she reached the first landing.

'Natalie?'

The sensual way he said her name had her turning to him instinctively, but she refused to go back, refused to be drawn into something neither of them wanted—or needed. She couldn't respond, couldn't say one word as their eyes met.

'*Grazie.*'

She didn't wait to find out what he thanking her for or even acknowledge it. She gave him a brief smile before she turned, forgetting her earlier intention and running up the stairs as fast as she could in her high heels. She didn't dare stop, not until she'd reached the sanctuary of her room.

Xavier woke as a chill spread over him. The fire, which had burned so hot at midnight, was now nothing more than embers glowing amidst the ash. Unfortunately, the same couldn't be said about the fire of desire within him.

He should never have kissed her, never have accepted her unspoken invitation to taste those lush lips, because now that he had, he wanted more. With each passing hour he'd been drawn to her with an inevitability that he'd been unable to ignore, despite the guilt that had prevented him from even thinking of kissing a woman in the last three years.

He stood up and pain niggled down his legs, a legacy of the accident and a constant reminder of his guilt. As was Tilly's insistence that she worked for him, making it plain that, despite the pull of attraction between them, nothing would ever happen.

But something had happened.

She'd kissed him back, responded so hotly he'd wanted her right there and then.

He'd only intended to brush his lips over hers in a celebratory kiss, and he'd almost stopped, sensing that a boundary would be crossed, a boundary she'd firmly set.

As his lips had tasted hers he'd lost his ability to think. The heat of her lips on his still seared him. Kissing her had been all he'd wanted to do; he couldn't allow things to go further, and not just because she was vulnerable. The only woman to have seen his battered body was Carlotta. As the memories of her revulsion had mixed with his constant guilt, he'd pushed Tilly away.

He'd watched Tilly all but run upstairs and had been unable to process the implications of what had happened. Her door had clicked closed and he had marched away from the ever-mocking Christmas tree, back to the heat of the fire.

Maledizione. He should never have kissed her. She'd tested his control, pushing it almost to the breaking point. He'd forced himself to let her go, to step away from her when every nerve in his body had cried out for the satisfaction of feeling her against him. He'd remained downstairs because he'd known Natalie wasn't a one-night sort of woman.

He glanced out of the landing windows, out into the night, which was illuminated by the snow, casting an eerie glow. At least it had stopped snowing. With any luck the minor roads leading away from the manor would be clear by tomorrow and she could leave—even if he had to dig through the snow to make a track to the road. She couldn't stay here, not when she tempted him, making him want things he had no right to want.

As he finally retired to his room he paused at the end of the corridor that led to Tilly's room. He imagined her asleep in the grand four-poster bed and knew he didn't want her to be so far away from him, and not just because they were alone in the house.

With another stream of curses muttered under his breath he turned and strode towards his room. Whatever had happened tonight could not be repeated.

CHAPTER FIVE

Tᴉʟʟʏ ᴡᴏᴋᴇ ᴡɪᴛʜ a start the next morning. At first she couldn't work out where she was. Then everything came flooding back. Had she really kissed Xavier last night? Or had it been a dream? Surely she hadn't done anything so stupid? She scanned the dim room, looking for anything that would remind her and help her clarify reality from dreams.

Her gaze rested on the black silk dress she'd draped over the chair last night and she closed her eyes in resignation as her memory cleared. She had kissed him. She'd thought he would be her fling, but she'd been unable to do it.

Her cheeks burned as the scene played out again in her mind. She could hear his deep sexy voice as they'd stood in the lounge, telling her that her contract was almost over. He'd used a celebratory New Year kiss to get past her guard. But celebration had definitely not been on her mind as she'd very daringly responded to him. After making it clear she was here in a professional capacity, she had been the one who'd taken it too far.

With her mind in turmoil, she slipped from the bed and pulled aside the heavy curtains, the cold from the leaded windows making her shiver, but at least it wasn't snowing. Hopefully she could try and get to Vanessa's house today. She had to be at the engagement party. There was no way she wanted to upset her friend, make her feel guilty for finding love and happiness, even if it did nudge at her own failings. More importantly she had to get away from the man who'd opened up the door to thoughts she should never have had.

She took clean jeans and a jumper from the case, wishing she'd had the forethought to put them to warm on the radiator last night. Almost haphazardly, she tossed everything else back into the case before closing it and turned her attention to the dress. Whatever had made her dash out and choose such a garment? As she'd put it on last night she'd really wanted Xavier to notice her and now she blushed at that idea.

Leaving the case and her dress, packed into its garment cover, on her bed, ready for a quick getaway, she left the room. A heavy silence filled the house as she walked along the corridor to the stairs, each window she passed offering a gorgeous view of the snowy parkland, but she didn't have time for that. She needed to pack her catering things and load the van—getting to Vanessa's engagement party was her priority.

She looked at the Christmas tree as she came to the bottom of the stairs, its bright decorations mocking her. For the second year in a row New Year's Eve had been a disaster. Both times it had been her fault. Either passion, or lack of it, had completely messed things up.

Walking down the corridor to the kitchen, she felt a blast of icy air and seeing the back door wide open went to close it, but not before she'd surveyed the depth of the snow and ascertained if there was any hope of getting her van out.

It looked unlikely. Snow had been driven by the wind, banking up against the wall of the courtyard and almost along one entire side of her van. Xavier's sporty number, so covered in snow it was unrecognisable, would most definitely not be going anywhere.

Large footprints trailed through the white blanket of snow, towards one of the stone outbuildings on the opposite side of the courtyard. What was Xavier doing?

As if conjured up by her thoughts, he emerged from the barn, his arms full of logs. He looked as if he was preparing to stay for a long time. Did he not want to rush back to London? He paused briefly when he saw her. '*Buon giorno*, Natalie.'

How could he sound so…? She struggled for the right word. Unaffected? After last night she had no idea how to act with him. How did you greet a man when you had all but thrown yourself at him the night before?

'Are you staying here longer?' Puzzlement filled her voice as she stood back to let him past, trying to ignore the heat building in her cheeks.

He stacked the logs against the wall just inside the back door, adding to those he must have already brought in. He didn't pause in his task, but the firmness of his voice warned her against disagreement. '*We* are staying longer.'

'We?' she gasped the word out in shock. 'I can't stay here. Not with you. Not after last night.'

He straightened, wiped his hands against each other and looked down at her, irritation plainly etched on his face. Suddenly the narrow passageway between the back door and the kitchen felt far too claustrophobic. He overpowered her completely. The scent of his aftershave nudged at memories of last night.

'Unless you want to dig out your van and the mile or so of driveway then, yes, *we* are staying.' There wasn't a trace of the gentleness she'd heard in his voice last night. She should be glad of that, but it still hurt to think he could kiss her so tenderly then just hours later almost dismiss her. It had been nothing more than just a New Year kiss, as he'd told her. One already forgotten—by him at least.

'But if I could get to the road…' she began, then, as his lips formed a hard line and he shook his head, she went on, 'The road is clear, isn't it?'

'It is no different from what you can see from the windows at the front of the house,' he added grimly. Was he too finding it hard to deal with the knowledge they could be marooned here for another day? Or was it the thought of being with a woman who'd launched herself at him so blatantly when all he'd wanted had been an uncomplicated New Year kiss? Could any kiss be uncomplicated?

'What about the main road?' Hope lifted

once more but was soon dashed by the quick shake of his head.

'I didn't get that far.'

'You went out?' She looked again at him, taking more notice of the boots he wore and the windproof jacket.

'I walked to the gates, yes.' He moved towards the kitchen and she let out a small breath of relief before following him. 'I went to see if we could leave and get back to London before the storm hits.'

'Storm? But I thought the snow we had overnight was the blizzard you mentioned yesterday.' Every nerve in her body was on high alert and she tried to tell herself it was because of the word 'storm' and nothing at all to do with the man himself or the way his dark eyes watched her.

'Last night was just snow. We are due to have blizzard conditions and the weather warnings have been upgraded.' He pulled out his phone, accessing the weather app. 'Blizzard conditions due to sweep across Britain today, causing massive disruption. Travel only if essential.'

'But...' she began, now at a total loss for words until finally her worst fears came out almost as a squeak. 'What if we are here for days?'

'*Va bene.*' He shrugged casually and then leant back against the kitchen unit, folding his arms across his chest. The action gave him domination of the entire room, as well as her thoughts. 'We have plenty of food. We are warm and safe. Better to stay here, no?'

No, she wanted to scream at him. It wasn't okay. She had to get to Vanessa's. She needed to be at that party. Vanessa had been there for her when her life had been turned upside down and now she *had* to be there for Vanessa, celebrating her friend's engagement, even if it was the last thing she wanted to do. On top of that she didn't want to be trapped in the countryside, snow all around, with a man who'd awakened something deep and unexpected within her. Especially as he was so unaffected by what had happened last night.

'I have to go. I can't stay here,' she began, disbelief washing over her, making coherent thought difficult.

'You do not have much choice, *cara*.' He raised a self-assured brow, seeming almost amused by her reaction.

'I can't stay here—with you—after last night.' She heard the words hiss from her lips and hated herself for the loss of control he'd provoked.

'Because you kissed me?'

'I did not kiss you.' Indignation at his blatant comment made her words sharp.

'You very definitely kissed me.' The smoothness of his accented voice sparked on her nerves like flint against steel, then he laughed as she glared at him. 'You have nothing to fear from me, Natalie.'

How could he say she had nothing to fear from him? Kissing him last night had changed everything—for her at least.

'I was working for you. You hired me to cater for your New Year's Eve dinner.' Her firm voice couldn't hide the confusion that raged inside her.

'And that is what you did, yes?' He was mocking her, making fun of her for reading anything into a kiss he'd clearly forgotten all about.

'Yes,' she snapped, heat infusing her cheeks.

'Then I see no problem. I contracted you to cater for New Year's Eve and your contract was completed even before the stroke of midnight.'

The outrage at his assumption sent her mind into turmoil, as did the knowledge he was right. She had completed her contract. She was no longer here in a professional capacity. 'That doesn't change anything.'

* * *

Xavier shrugged. He'd enjoyed the kiss last night, maybe even a little too much, but was he ready to get involved with another woman, especially one who wanted the full package, the happy-ever-after? Since the accident he'd only dated women, never going beyond dinner, unable to deal with their almost certain revulsion at his scarring.

He sensed Tilly was different and had tested the boundaries she'd set. She may have kissed him back, may have been tempted by the passion that burned like glowing embers between them, but the fact she'd fled last night had given him a very clear message. She was off limits, he should heed that, instead of taking it as a challenge. He wasn't the man he used to be.

'I still can't stay here—alone with you, Xavier. People will talk.' A hint of resignation lingered in those last words and he knew she was right. People would gossip and make assumptions.

'Does it really matter what people say?' He stepped towards her and saw her eyes widen, saw the doubt and anxiety in them.

'I'm not forcing you to stay, Natalie. Go if that's what you have to do.' He stepped back.

He wasn't going to make her do anything. Stay or go. It was a decision she had to make for herself.

'It doesn't look as if I have any choice in the matter. I'm going to have to stay here.' She snapped the words out, agitation in every step as she walked back towards the kitchen.

He turned in the doorway and looked at her, annoyed by the look of devastation on her face. Was spending time with him that bad? 'Very well, *cara*. I will fetch more logs for the fire.'

'That sounds like you expect us to be here for days.' Her big blue eyes widened with incredulity.

'At my home in the Italian mountains, if bad weather is forecast it is sensible to make such preparations.' He opened the door, about to go back to the outbuildings, the chill from outside cooling the ardour that just thinking of her kiss infused through him.

'We are not in the Italian mountains.' Irritation rang out of every syllable and she fixed him with a fierce glare.

'This is true, but the forecast is not good, so indulge me in this at least, *cara*.' He injected light humour into his voice and was rewarded with the smallest of smiles, the irritation of moments ago seemingly forgotten. Her lips, which had felt so good against his last night, lifted fractionally.

'Do what you feel necessary. I'm going to check the forecast for myself.' The brashness of her voice as she picked up her phone from the neat pile of paperwork wasn't lost on him, but he couldn't resist the urge to provoke more of a reaction from her.

'Don't you trust me?' The question hung between them as once again he came under her scrutiny.

'Actually, no, I don't.' The matter-of-fact reply shocked him and if he were truthful, he would admit the same. He shouldn't be trusted, not after her kiss had begun to melt his stern control. He didn't trust himself. It would be wise to step back from whatever it was arcing between them. It was something he wasn't ready for.

'*Va bene, cara.* You check the weather, reassure yourself I'm telling the truth and not keeping you here for my own pleasure. While you do that I'll fetch more logs.' He turned and left through the back door, welcoming the cool air against his face.

It had started to snow again as he crossed the courtyard and the sky was heavy and ominously grey. Tilly didn't need to look up more weather forecasts—she should just step outside, feel the icy wind and see the snow beginning to fall again.

As he loaded the basket with logs he kept his mind on the weather. Allowing it to wander elsewhere would mean going back to the moment last night just before he'd kissed her. The moment he'd stopped, reminding himself she wasn't one of his usual female companions.

She was different—and he'd known that from the first moment he'd seen her, but he'd lost reason and given in to the need to feel her lips beneath his. Any honourable intentions had evaporated as she'd responded, instantly firing the desire that had simmered inside him.

Smettila! No good would come of replaying that moment over and over. He had to stay resolved to the fact it had meant nothing. Hundreds of people would have shared a kiss at midnight on New Year's Eve.

But would it have been a kiss like that?

'Maledizione!' He cursed as he filled the log basket, hurling them in harder than was necessary. Never had he known a woman to affect him so much. Why did it have to be this one and why now?

Snow was falling steadily as he made his

way back to the house, content that if the worst happened and they lost power, as was often the case at his mountain home, they would be warm.

He tried to push all his thoughts away, lock them behind a door and return to the professional relationship she had worked hard to maintain. But that kiss lingered in his mind and a hot burning need streaked through him. They had been warm last night. Too warm.

As he closed the back door against the swirling snow, she came into the hall, her phone still in her hand, a worried frown creasing her brow. If he could give in to the instinct of protection, he'd wrap his arms around her and tell her it would be all right, but he couldn't allow that temptation.

'You were right,' she said, the heated tone of her words letting him know it hurt to admit that. 'I've rung Vanessa and she said the roads are bad there and insisted that I should stay here.'

'And are you?' He watched the worry and panic filter across her face, wishing he could smooth them away with a kiss.

'Am I what?' The question snapped at him, revealing much more of her fear than he thought she'd like him to know.

'Going to stay here?'

'I don't have much choice about it.'

He stifled a smile and adopted an air of aloofness. 'In that case, I suggest making up the fire in the small lounge for this evening.'

'The small lounge?'

'It is where I was working yesterday and is much smaller. If the electricity fails, it will be warmer.' He carried the log basket along the corridor and out into the main hallway. The damn Christmas tree still mocked him with its merriment. If they stayed here much longer, he'd be forced to do something about that. Every time he saw it he imagined those children having Christmas after Christmas without their father.

He forced the dark thoughts of Paulo from his mind and went into the small lounge. He knew she'd followed him. He could feel it with every nerve in his body but pushed away the pulse of desire as it began to move through him.

'Wouldn't going to bed be warmer?' The innocent question rocked his senses, sending them spiralling into overdrive.

He put down the basket on the hearth of the fireplace and looked at Tilly as a blush spread across her cheeks. The kick of lust that burst through him at the thought of her in his bed and in his arms made a response to such an innocent comment almost impossible.

'Alone,' she added firmly, before he could muster his response.

'Sitting here together, in front of a fire, will be much warmer and far more sociable, no?'

'Not very professional, though,' she added with a haughty rise of her brows that verged on flirtatious.

'I thought we'd settled this. You are no longer here in an official capacity.' He moved towards her, drawn by the memory of her lips against his. 'Your contract was completed once dinner was over last night. You are now my guest.'

Tilly could hardly think for the pounding of her heart. Did he have to move so close, remind her of the kiss she'd responded to?

'I—I still have work to do,' she stammered, and stepped away from him, away from the temptation of inhaling his heady masculine scent. 'I have things to pack away, and if we are going to be here tonight we'll need to eat, so I am still working for you.'

She knew she was talking too much, that her jumble of thoughts would probably sound incoherent. Jason had always told her she talked too much when she was nervous. Jason. The name dropped into her mind like a large stone into a rock pool, sending all previous thoughts out in a huge splash.

At least it focused her mind. It didn't matter how much she was attracted to Xavier, he wasn't what she needed in life. The last thing she wanted was a man renowned for working hard and playing even harder.

'You are now my guest, Natalie, but if it makes you feel better, *va bene.*'

His voice was deep and those Italian words not only set her heart racing but tugged at precious memories from long ago. They became as clear as if they'd happened yesterday—her grandmother cooking, her parents happy together. All that had been before her father's illness, before her childhood had been shattered by his death.

With the weight of the past pressing down on her, she forced her mind back to the present, her voice sharper than she'd intended. 'It does make me feel better, so I'll leave you to do the caveman job and light the fire.' Before he could say anything she strode purposefully from the room. Time away from the aura of power he exuded was necessary if her heart rate was to return to anything like normal.

As she left the room she heard the low rumble of his laugh and marvelled that she could find it so sexy, so appealing when he was clearly mocking her, entertaining himself at her expense.

Xavier's charm was lethal if nothing else. Anywhere else she could walk away, but stuck here in this rambling old house, cocooned from the real world, it was different—very different and very dangerous.

'Don't fall for his charm,' she berated herself angrily, as she continued to pack away her catering equipment, certain that first thing tomorrow she would be on the way to see Vanessa before returning to London and reality. This surreal interlude would be over, forgotten and dismissed.

CHAPTER SIX

ALL AFTERNOON TILLY had tried to ignore the falling snow, knowing that with each flake the likelihood she and Xavier would be alone here for several days increased. The chance of leaving the manor had slipped away as fast as the daylight and now she was faced with another night in Xavier's company.

The ringing of her phone gave her yet another excuse to linger in the kitchen. 'Tilly? Are you all right?' Vanessa's voice reconnected her to the outside world.

'I'm fine.' She injected laughter into her voice in an attempt to put Vanessa's mind at rest. 'Trapped in a beautiful manor house with an incredibly sexy Italian man, of course I'm all right.'

'We've postponed the party until next week. I really want you there, Tilly.'

'I will be,' Tilly reassured her. 'I promise.'

'I have to go now, but you just remember

that one big item on your bucket list. This could be your chance, Tilly. Don't waste it.'

'Vanessa, behave yourself and get back to your fiancé.' Tilly ended the call, still smiling at her friend's very unsubtle advice, but Vanessa had only echoed what had already crossed her mind several times.

Thankfully Xavier was still ensconced in the small lounge with his paperwork. She prepared supper and was pleasantly surprised to find he'd opened a bottle of red wine when she took the food into him. They ate in companionable silence and Vanessa's advice rattled around in her head as loudly as the wind around the old manor house. Tilly sipped her wine, reluctantly feeling calmer as she sat on the sofa before the fire, lulled by its heat and the comforting glow of the flames.

'This is much nicer than the grandeur of the lounge,' she said, looking around her, taking in the desk by the windows that Xavier had been working at all afternoon, his briefcase open, papers spilling out.

'*Sì*, it is cosy but, more importantly, much warmer.' He looked at her, his dark eyes holding a message she couldn't resist.

She blushed at his words, concentrating on the orange flames as they curled around the logs. She tried to change the subject, keep away from stirring the tension that sizzled around them constantly. 'The wind is getting worse.'

The lights dimmed, flickered then came back. She looked at Xavier, who didn't appear at all perturbed, and forced herself to relax back into the moment she'd just been pulled from.

The lights flickered again and the howl of the wind sounded like a forlorn and lonely animal from the moors. Stop being so dramatic, she told herself sharply, but her anxiety level rose as Xavier got up and lit one of the large white pillar candles that adorned the mantelpiece.

'The power could go out.' He focused his attention on lighting more of the candles.

Was the weather due to be that bad? A trickle of fear ran down her spine and staying in Xavier's company suddenly became a whole lot more appealing. He wouldn't abandon her if the lights went out, would he?

'Surely that won't happen,' she said quickly and a little too sharply, forcing those memories back. Now was not the time to remember the misery of her childhood after her father had died or how Jason had walked out on her so casually.

'In case you hadn't noticed, Natalie, we are in rural Devon, on the edge of Exmoor. I would strongly suspect power cuts are more than normal in this kind of weather.'

His matter-of-fact deduction irritated her and again she studied the leaping flames of the fire, anything other than look from his broad shoulders all the way down to his long legs. Every bit of him was attractive and that spark fizzed in her once more as she remembered being in his arms last night. She could still feel the heat of his touch as he'd caressed her slumbering body awake. Vanessa's advice rushed back. *This could be your chance, Tilly.* Could she abandon her fears for just one night?

What was she thinking?

'In that case, thank you for lighting the candles.' What was the matter with her? The tartness of her voice positively prickled with challenge—something you didn't do with a man such as Xavier Moretti.

The lights flickered then went off and the glow of the fire and the candlelight surrounded him as he turned to her. It was then she was aware she'd given a startled gasp. She looked up into his face as he laughed softly.

'You were saying, *cara*?' He sounded so different when he laughed, as if it was something he wasn't familiar with.

'Okay,' she conceded, and raised her glass to him, desperate to hide the emotions that were being unlocked. 'You win.'

He picked up the bottle of wine and poured more into her glass, then his, before sitting on the sofa. He touched his glass against hers, the sound strangely loud. 'To my win.'

No sooner had he said the words than the lights flickered back on. 'Maybe not.' The lightness of her voice almost betrayed her relief and he looked at her questioningly. The gurgle of laughter that threatened to rise from her left her in no doubt she shouldn't drink much more wine, but right now, despite preserving her ideals of professionalism, she was happy to be in Xavier's company.

'What would you have been doing this evening, at the party?' The question, asked in such a deep and accented voice, caught her attention and she looked at him, unaware of just how close he was now sitting to her, until she looked into his eyes.

She tried to break eye contact, tried to prevent him from looking deep into her soul, but she couldn't. She was compelled by something she'd never known before. 'I felt so guilty about not being there, but it has been postponed until next week. I promised that, whatever happened, I will be there. I don't want Vanessa to think I'm hiding behind excuses.'

'Why would she think you are hiding, Natalie?' His sexy voice rose questioningly, his dark gaze holding hers.

'Hiding?' She hated the way her voice rose, but didn't miss the slight narrowing of his eyes. 'I'm not hiding. I wanted this New Year to be different from any other. I guess I was trying to prove to my family and friends that I'd put the past behind me and moved on.'

'But you haven't, have you, *cara*? Not completely.'

What was going on here? It was as if all her past hurt was being dragged out for inspection, forced out by this man and the situation they were in. 'It's hard to forget the humiliation of being stood up just hours before your wedding.'

'But you are still in love with this man?'

She wasn't in love with Jason, not the way she should have been, she realised with a jolt. She'd been in love with the idea of companionship and their longstanding friendship. She'd thought she'd found her happy-ever-after with a trusted and safe friend. It was only now she realised that all along she'd been afraid to love; she hadn't wanted to be like her mother, constantly searching for something so elusive it almost destroyed her.

The day her father had died, her relationship with her mother had changed, leaving her emotionally alone. A gap soon filled by Jason's friendship. He had been patient, never pressuring her to make it physically more, so the fact he'd found that somewhere else only added to her pain.

She shook her head in denial. 'He is about to get married. After telling me he wanted freedom to live life to the full.'

Indignation at the revelations he'd made to her about wanting more than just friendship came flooding back. She knew then she'd lost a friend as well as a fiancé. Sadness had been in his eyes as he'd told her he wanted more than friendship and he'd fallen into an affair.

'He'd said we should go out and find life, live it to the full, make the most of every opportunity.'

'Did you?' He watched her intently but she looked into the leaping orange flames of the fire.

'Yes, I made a list of all the things I wanted

to do.' She'd responded with more information than she'd intended, the ability to talk to him like this as unnerving as it was liberating.

'So…' He moved fractionally closer. 'What is on this list?'

'To make my business successful.' She felt her cheeks redden as she thought of how she'd contemplated a romantic fling with him. 'I only started it in the spring.'

'That I think is being achieved. Anything else?'

'To go back to Italy and find my father's family. We lost touch when he died.'

'Nothing exciting or different? What about something for you? Something you'd like to do that would change you or your life?' His words were velvety smooth and she couldn't look at him, knowing how close he was to the truth that he could be on the list.

'I'd like to go to America and ride a cowboy trail, and do something spontaneous.' She couldn't say that something was to have a romantic fling or that she was seriously considering it right now.

He nodded in approval and the pounding of her heart and the wail of the wind seemed louder. She couldn't help herself but look into the darkness of Xavier's eyes, the sizzle of something powerful sparking between them. He'd admitted to pushing his girlfriend away after the accident and she knew he'd had a constant string of women in his life since he'd arrived in London. He was worse than Jason, discarding a woman without a second thought.

The question was on the tip of her tongue when the lights went out. No warning flickers this time. Thank goodness for the candles. She didn't think she could tolerate darkness now, not when her past had been dragged up for inspection.

'I'll go and check the fuses,' he said as he stood up, the candlelight softening the usually hard angle of his face. 'But I suspect the storm is responsible.'

'How long will you be?' The little girl in her surfaced and she fought to keep the tremor from her voice.

'Not long.' He picked his phone up from the table, turned on its torch and looked at her, concern in his eyes. Was that for her or the situation? 'Stay here.'

Tilly had no intention of venturing away from the candlelight and listened to his footsteps as he crossed the wooden floor of the hallway, feeling more alone than she ever had.

The old house wasn't warm and welcoming any more and the pain of last New Year's Eve lurked in all the dark corners.

She moved from the sofa and sat down on the rug in front of the fire, needing the warmth of the leaping flames, wanting to feel the heat on her face, needing it to stop herself from thinking too much.

Xavier pushed open the door to find Tilly sitting on the floor, one arm pulling her knees tight against her body as she sat in front of the fire. She looked gorgeous. An innocent vulnerability radiated from her and the urge to protect her, to keep her safe from whatever fears she was hiding from him, welled up in him.

She looked up at him as he closed the door. 'The power is definitely off,' he offered, as he made his way to the fire, throwing on another few logs. 'The blizzard must have brought down power lines.'

'Is it that bad out there?' She shivered and he reached for the faux fur throw that was draped over the sofa.

Her eyes widened as he moved towards her, vulnerability on full display in their blue depths. Every barrier she'd erected against him was down. This was the real Tilly.

'This will keep you warm.' He put the throw around her and couldn't help but inhale her perfume. Light and floral, not at all like the seductive scent of last night, but it was just as alluring.

'Thank you,' she whispered, the husky sound testing him, reminding him again how she'd tasted last night, how her body had felt against his. The frustration of last night not having reached the conclusion he'd wanted raged inside him, but he pushed it back. He had no right to want more from her.

He sat down next to her, ignoring the pain in his legs, wanting to be close to her. The usually bubbly Tilly had disappeared. She was fearful and he was convinced it was more than just the storm she feared.

'You're in pain,' she said softly, concern all over her face.

'A constant reminder of the accident.' He couldn't keep the sternness from his voice as he tried not to remember his split-second lack of concentration that had caused the crash.

'Sorry.' She looked up at him from beneath lowered lashes, her blue eyes soft and inviting. He curled his hands into fists to stop himself from reaching for her. He needed the pain to remind him that his actions had caused Paulo's death, leaving a widow and young children. He didn't need her misplaced sympathy.

He sat next to her, the heat of the fire seeping into him as if he were on a sun-drenched beach. He stretched out his legs and leant his back against the sofa. Beside him, Tilly moved, drawing herself closer, as if seeking protection and safety from the darkness. She rested her head on his shoulder and he put his arm around her, drawing her close. It felt so right, as if he'd come home.

'How did the accident happen?' Her voice was a whisper, stirring his senses as well as soothing his pain.

He didn't want her to know what he'd done, but for the first time ever he needed to tell someone, needed to talk. 'It was a wet race,' he began, sliding back into the horror of that day. 'The track was slick and like most riders I'd had my tyres changed. The team wanted to make other adjustments but I wouldn't allow it, not when all the other riders were out there. Part of the excitement is being in the starting lineup, engines revving and adrenalin flowing.'

She didn't speak or look at him, as if knowing he didn't want that. Instead she relaxed against his chest and focused her gaze on the fire. He lowered his face into her hair and inhaled the fresh smell of shampoo. But even that couldn't hold him in the present, stop him from hurtling back to that nightmare day.

He was there at the track, the noise of bikes, the smell of fuel and the rush of adrenalin so clear. The usual exchanges between teammates filled the air and in the pit lane he waited for those adjustments to his bike. He wanted to get out into the line-up, but the mechanics were still working and he became impatient. His competitors revved their bikes, the sound a challenge. He told his team to hurry.

'I rushed the pit team to hurry the wet-weather modifications just so I could get out onto the track. There was no way I was missing the race, not when the championship was at stake.'

Tilly moved slightly, picked up her glass of wine and took a sip, shattering the image of the track in his mind. She looked up at him, her lovely face slightly flushed from the heat of the fire. What would she say when she knew it was his fault a rider had died, because of him and his insistence the bike be ready to race?

She was so close he could see the darker flecks within the summer sky blue of her eyes, which had sparked with passion last night. He could feel the warmth of her legs against his as she curled up inside the throw, snuggling closer, unwittingly testing him.

He wanted to keep her against him, needing the comfort of her body and so much more.

'Aren't things like that strictly timed?' she asked, her brows raised in question, genuine curiosity in her voice. 'I was always under the impression the pit teams were trained to be fast.'

'Do I detect a little bit of interest in motorcycle racing?' He smiled at her, despite the heavy cloud of memories which hung over him.

'Not really, sorry.' Her smile was apologetic as she looked up at him, but it shone in her eyes briefly before it was gone. 'Jason used to follow all kinds of motorsport.'

Jason again. Damn the man.

'I'm sorry.' She placed her glass on the hearth and touched his arms, which were tightly folded across his chest. Was that to avoid touching her or to keep her at bay—emotionally? 'Talking about the accident must be hard.'

'It is.' He seized on the deviation in the conversation. 'My career ended that day and my life changed—for ever.'

'But you are doing so much good with the scholarship programme.' She looked into his face, drawing him from the blackness of the mood that lingered with more threat than the gale-force winds outside the manor house.

'You know about that?'

She blushed deeply. 'Naturally I research my clients.'

His lips stiffened into a firm line. How much more did she know about him? 'And did you find your research adequate?'

'I didn't look for salacious gossip if that's what you mean.'

'You mean the sort of gossip we are creating at this very moment, alone in a remote house?'

He moved forward, drawn by those very kissable lips, wanting nothing more than to feel them beneath his again. She didn't move, her gaze holding his, questions and anticipation swirling within them.

'Are we creating gossip?' Her husky whisper nearly tipped him over the edge and it was all he could do not to kiss her until neither of them wanted to stop.

'There isn't anyone here to say a word to the outside world.' He searched her face, looking for a hint of the desire that flowed like hot lava through his body. 'Nobody will ever know what we do.'

She glanced at the flickering candles, then back to him. 'It's like being in another time or place, somewhere reality can't reach.'

Tentatively, as if he were reaching for a skittish animal, he caressed her face, the backs of his fingers brushing down the softness of her cheek. 'We are surrounded by darkness, nothing can reach us.'

'It's a little scary being in this old house on such a stormy night.' The cracked whisper almost broke his control, but he managed to resist the urge to hold her against him, to kiss and caress away her fears.

'There is nothing to fear, *cara*.' He pushed her hair back gently from her face, relishing the thick glossy length falling through his fingers.

Those blue eyes searched his face briefly but as his hand pressed against the back of her head, his fingers tangling in her hair, she moved towards him. He saw her eyelashes flutter closed and then his lips were against hers, the electrifying pulse racing through him. With a groan of pleasure he wrapped the other arm around her, pulling her against him so that she was almost on his legs.

He could feel the heat of her body, every curve pressing into him, reawakening the need she'd stirred last night. One so strong he'd never known anything like it before.

He wanted her—tonight.

Tilly sighed as he deepened the kiss and pulled her close. She knew she shouldn't surrender to his kiss, as she had done last night. His reassurance that she had nothing to fear had pushed her over an edge she realised she'd been balancing on, not just since last night but since the moment she'd seen him standing in the doorway yesterday, looking so sexy and mildly amused. It had been almost like love at first sight. Not that she thought such a thing was possible, not with a man like Xavier, but what was possible was a romantic fling. All she had to do was let go of her insecurities, be someone else, be spontaneous, free herself of her fear of passion and give herself to this man—just for one night.

That was what she wanted, what she needed. To be kissed by him, held by him, but more than that she wanted to be loved by him just for one night. Tonight they were in another world, a place far away from time and untouched by reality.

As that thought meandered through her mind, Xavier's groan of pleasure sent sparks flying around her body and the mesmerising throb of desire that was building deep inside her began to bubble up, leaving her in no doubt where this moment would end.

'You taste so delicious, *cara*.' He pressed a flurry of tantalising kisses down her throat, hindered by her roll neck jumper, and pressed her forehead against his, her hair mingling with his. If she tasted delicious, he smelt it.

She let out a ragged and startled breath as he took her face between both of his hands, forcing her to look deep into his desire-laden eyes. 'This moment was meant for us, *bella* Natalie. *Questo momento è per noi.*'

His husky and heavy accent together with the use of Italian sealed her fate. All she wanted was to throw caution to the wailing wind and abandon herself to him and the moment, to let go of everything and do what she wanted without a thought for what would come after. She wanted to love Xavier, in every possible way. Tonight she was his—and he was hers.

'Xavier.' She whispered his name, unsure if it was a question or a demand. She should tell him, warn him she had no experience, that she was a virgin, but his eyes met hers, so dark she thought she would drown in them, and she couldn't say anything.

His lips claimed hers, hard and demanding, sending fire scorching through her, and she wrapped her arms around his neck, responding with a need she'd never known before. This wasn't the staid kisses she'd shared with Jason. This was pure explosive passion.

His tongue slid into her mouth, seeking hers. It was wild and erotic. The pulse of wanton desire rose inside her and she craved more, so much more. She matched his passion, her tongue entwining with his until she thought she might burst into flames.

He pushed her down onto the rug, the rumpled throw beneath her, but she kept her arms around his neck, pulling him with her until she could feel him pressing against her. His chest, which expanded with deep and fast breaths, pressed against her breasts and with one leg between hers she could feel the hardness of his erection against her thigh.

Every nerve ending in her body responded as she enjoyed the sensation of being in his arms, being kissed by him. He stopped kissing her and, brushing her hair away from her face, looked down at her. 'I want you, Natalie, and, I'm not going to be able to stop if I continue to kiss you like this.' The words were thick with passion, a hint of unsteadiness in them.

'Then kiss me.' The husky whisper that came from her was something she'd never heard before but, then, she'd never been so consumed by passion before. The whole experience was new and exciting. She'd never been intimate with a man and had had no idea it could be like this. 'Kiss me, Xavier.'

The fierceness of the last kiss was gone, replaced now by something more gentle yet infinitely more exciting. As his lips teased hers, his hand slid under her jumper, the heat of his touch on her skin so extreme she gasped in a startled breath. His kiss deepened, his tongue entwining with hers as his hand covered her breast, his fingers trailing along the edge of her bra, making her breasts ache for his touch.

He moved himself down her body and kissed her exposed stomach, pushing her jumper ever higher until all she wanted was to feel his kisses on her breasts, tasting each hardened peak. She closed her eyes against the pleasure, a soft sigh of contentment slipping between her lips as he continued to tease her, kissing lower, nearing the fastening of her jeans.

It was exquisite.

She pushed herself into a sitting position and he looked at her, his passion filled eyes holding a question. She couldn't speak, but instead took the bottom of her jumper and lifted up her arms, bringing the black roll neck over her head. She dropped it at her side and partially unclothed in jeans and a black bra, boldly stayed there as his hungry gaze devoured her.

'Sei una bella donna.' Each wonderfully sexy word was more like a harsh growl and she knew he was hanging onto his control by a thread. It excited and amazed her to think she was responsible. This was definitely spontaneous.

He moved towards her, kissed her lips then down her throat. She leant back on her arms, her head dropping back as his kisses moved downwards. Her heart hammered when he moved lower and kissed the swell of first one breast then the other. It was so nice she began to shake.

'You are cold?' He stopped and looked at her, concern obvious in his face.

'No, I'm not cold,' she sighed. She wasn't cold, just afraid of what she was about to do, even though she wanted it more than anything.

He smiled knowingly at her, but glanced at the fire. 'A few more logs will keep us warmer for longer, no?'

She didn't need the fire to keep her warm, not when the one he'd started was raging inside her. As he moved away, she watched him, wanting nothing more than to see his body, feel his skin against hers. The thought sent her pulse racing.

He put more logs on the fire, coaxing the flames until they leapt in a crazy dance, licking around the wood. She was just like those pieces of wood, becoming totally engulfed by the scorching flames of desire.

This wasn't at all what she'd thought she would be doing tonight. Never had she imagined she'd be enjoying the caress of a man who could make her pulse leap with just one casual glance. A romantic fling might be on her list, but she'd never thought it would happen, never believed she could really go through with it.

'That's quite a fire now,' she teased as he turned back to her, the intention of moments ago still lingering in his expression. 'Looks like we will be here for some time.'

His gaze travelled down her, making her skin tingle as if he'd touched her. 'I have every intention of being here with you for as long as possible, *cara*.'

She watched as he walked around behind the sofa to the desk he'd been working at earlier. He opened his briefcase with a click and she heard papers being moved, then a box being opened.

His gaze met hers as he put a foil packet in his jeans pocket, his intention clear. This was her last chance to stop this. But she couldn't. Tonight she was his, all her inhibitions were banished. She needed this passion, wanted to taste it and savour it so it would last for ever.

She blushed, her boldness of moments ago evaporating like raindrops in the desert. As he came back to her and pulled off his jumper then his shirt, she swallowed hard. The glow from the fire bronzed his skin, highlighting his each and every muscle to complete perfection.

She bit down on her bottom lip, totally out of her depth. He was so passionately in control and she was a virgin. Would he know? Her hungry gaze roved all over his body, pushing away her doubts as her fingers ached to touch him. She noticed the livid scarring that started at his side and went down, hidden by the denim of his jeans.

Aware of him watching her, she looked back into his face. He looked at her suspiciously, his jaw clenched hard, and she struggled to find something to say to defuse the tension.

'I hope we'll be here all night like this,' she finally said softly, picking up the conversation where it had stopped before he'd stripped off to the waist.

He turned back to the fireplace and blew out the candles, leaving only the fire to light the room. A prickle of fear chased over her as his action unintentionally pushed her further out of her comfort zone.

'It's a bit dark.' Her heart was thudding in her chest and she couldn't decide if it was because of seeing Xavier semi-naked or the darkness he'd plunged them into.

'I only need firelight to see your beautiful body and it is so much more...' he pondered for a moment and she waited, not daring to move '...romantic?'

Did a man like Xavier do romantic? If her pulse wasn't racing so wildly and he wasn't moving towards her, passionate intent sparking in his eyes, she'd have said no. But right now nothing else mattered. She didn't care about the past, which lurked in every shadowed corner of the room, or the future, which she'd yet to discover. This was the romantic fling she needed to move on in life.

CHAPTER SEVEN

THE SMELL OF freshly extinguished candles
filled the room but all Xavier could think of
was taking Tilly in his arms, kissing her all
over, exploring every bit of her delicious body.
He wanted her naked beneath him as he made
her his.

She seemed nervous and he resolved to be
gentle, to coax out the desire he knew burned
within her and show her she was a beautiful
and passionate woman, sure that Jason's rejection would have filled her with self-doubt, an
emotion he knew well.

He knelt down next to her, a twinge of pain
in his leg reminding him, if he needed it, why
he preferred she didn't see him undressed
under bright lights. He had no wish to frighten
her further. He didn't want her running from
him, not tonight, not when he intended to take
what they'd started last night to its conclusion.
'What is wrong, *mia cara*?'

'Nothing,' she whispered huskily, as she knelt up and moved towards him. 'Not now.'

He took her in his arms, bringing her closer to him and in one swift movement pulled her to sit astride his legs, her arms around his neck, her breasts level with his face. He watched the soft swell of them moving up and down with each breath, resisting the urge to discard her bra and taste first one nipple then the other.

'There is no need to be afraid of anything, *cara*…' Instantly she tensed in his arms, her legs no longer relaxed and heavy against him. She was still resisting him, still reasoning over her actions when she should just give in to him and enjoy the night for what it was.

'Being here like this, with just the fire, it's not something I've done before.' She lowered her lashes, their long length sweeping down to spread over her cheeks. She was still hiding from him.

Gently he lifted her chin, forcing her to look at him. 'Would you like me to light the candles again?' He didn't want to do that. It would expose his scars, his hang-ups and fears. He was damn sure she wouldn't stay around once she saw the full horror of how badly scarred his legs were. She would be gone. For the first time in three years he was prepared to take the risk and make love to a woman, but that didn't mean he wanted her to see his scars.

'No. There's no need.' She shook her head slowly and began to relax. He felt her limbs soften and a burst of hot lust shot through him as she leant towards him. His fingers still held her chin and he guided her closer until their lips were almost touching—almost kissing.

'You look like a goddess in this light.' His husky whisper shuddered from him as he fought to hold his control, wanting to savour this moment. She was so different from all the women who virtually threw themselves at his feet with alarming regularity.

Tilly needed to be handled with care. She needed him to be gentle and considerate and the idea sent desire hurtling through him. She deserved more than a frantic tumble to satisfy a lust-filled moment but he was past rational thought now.

He felt her breath on his face, her body against his, and knew she wanted to be loved. She deserved to be, but he couldn't love her, not in that way. He shouldn't even be kissing her. But he wanted her, needed her, as if only she could breathe life back into his battered body and tortured soul.

'Right now, I feel like a goddess.' The gentle purr of her voice pushed his control to the breaking point and he claimed her lips in a hard and demanding kiss. His fingers slid into her hair, gripping it as he focused on keeping her where he wanted her, allowing him to deepen the kiss.

She lifted her head, a ragged gasp rushing from her, and he moved his attentions to the hardened peaks of her nipples, clearly visible through her bra.

'*Dio mio*, you are beautiful.' The throaty rasp of his voice almost broke as she took a deep breath in, her breasts moving closer to him, teasing him so much he began to question just who was in control. Her or him?

Heady lust hurtled through him as he pressed his lips against the creamy swell of one breast, feeling each deep breath she took and the thumping of her heart. His hand cupped the other, his thumb rubbing over her nipple as it strained against the lacy fabric covering it.

'Xavier.' The husky whisper of his name snapped that last thread of control and he let go of her hair, reached to the fastening of her bra and snapped it open, freeing each delectable breast for his attention.

Her fingers clutched at his hair as he kissed one nipple, teasing it until she was shuddering with desire, each breath she took as deep and ragged as his. His tongue swirled around it, tasting her.

'Too much,' she gasped between increasingly shallow breaths.

'Too much?' He pulled back from her and looked up at her flushed face. 'Should I stop, *cara*?'

'Yes. No. I don't know.' She sighed and looked down at him and he realised he'd nearly pushed her over the edge. It was as if she was discovering the joy of such pleasures for the first time, and had never sampled the delights of passion. 'No, don't. This is on my list.'

He puzzled over the words whispered in a throaty way that left him in no doubt she was losing the battle of resistance. 'This in on your list?'

'Yes, but don't stop.'

Her fingers curled tighter in his hair, pushing him to a new limit, and with gentleness he moved her from him, trying not to acknowledge the pain of having knelt on the floor, and pushed her down against the throw that was spread out over the rug.

She lay back, her gaze holding his all the time, a hint of a question lingering beneath the sparks of passion.

'We will take it slowly,' he said as he lowered his head and kissed the flatness of her stomach, his hands holding her waist. He straddled her as he moved upwards, tasting her with each kiss.

She clutched at his shoulders, her fingernails digging into his flesh. He moved higher still and once more kissed her breasts, nipping at the hardened peaks, relishing the gasps of pleasure that escaped those full lips.

He kissed a trail up her throat until he could once more claim her lips in a hard and demanding kiss. She pulled him down on top of her and wrapped her jeans-clad legs around his. The hardness of his erection strained against the confines of his jeans but he enjoyed the wild and erotic sensation of being partially clothed, of being able to feel her beneath him.

It was explosive. New and exciting.

Her hands slid down his back, her fingertips finding the beginnings of the scarring on his right side. He tensed as she paused briefly in her trail of exploration across his back. She hadn't uttered a word, hadn't asked the dreaded question. *How did this happen?* He pressed kisses over her face, the side of her neck and against her ears, thankful she hadn't broken the spell or killed the passion between them.

He wanted her naked, completely naked. He pushed back from her, kneeling up to unfasten her jeans. Her hair splayed out around her as she watched him, tempting and seducing him with her innocent eyes while lifting her hips to help. He moved back on his knees, pulling the denim and her slipper-like shoes away until she wore only a skimpy pair of black panties.

He groaned at the need to set himself free of his ever-tightening jeans. Her eyes, darker with each passing second, watched him intently, as if aware of his torture. They goaded him, urged him to remove every last barrier between them. But he couldn't. Not yet. He didn't want the battered part of his body to ruin the moment.

Instead, he turned his attention to giving her the pleasure she craved. He touched the black lace panties with the tip of one finger, moving down over her, the damp fabric arousing his ardour higher and higher.

She moved against him, testing his control beyond any limits he'd known before. He slipped his finger inside the damp black lace, teasing her heated flesh until she writhed against him. Within seconds she gasped as spasms of pleasure rocked her body. He ceased his teasing and ripped off his jeans and underwear as she lay, eyes closed in pleasure.

* * *

Tilly couldn't stop shaking. She'd lost all control of her body—and it was so good. In a faraway place she knew what it was, knew that for the first time she'd exploded with pleasure, from just a touch. A very expert and practised touch.

As the waves of passion ebbed over her she closed her eyes, unsure what to do next. She felt Xavier move away, heard the sound of denim dropping to the floor and with stars of ecstasy still in her head she couldn't do or say anything but tremble with lingering desire.

Seconds later Xavier was beside her, pulling the other throw over them. He was naked. Completely naked. The heated hardness of his erection pressed against her hip and she couldn't help the smile of contentment that tugged at her lips.

He wanted her. Desired her.

She turned towards him as he pulled her against him, the blackness of his eyes so intense, so full of unquenched desire she knew she was lost. He pressed himself against her, forcing a ragged breath through her lips, which he caught with a kiss so powerful she almost cried out.

Driven by something new and wild, she

pushed against him, rolling him onto his back, until she was over him, able the feel him close to her, almost touching yet not quite.

'Stuzzicare!' His eyes locked with hers and his jaw clenched as if he was desperately trying to stay in control.

'What does that mean?' The seductive whisper surprised even her and she pressed her fingertips against his stomach, tracing the arrow of dark hair downwards, wanting to use her new-found power over him and make him dissolve as rapidly as she had done from his touch.

'Tease!' He ground the word out as he fought against her need to rob him of all his self-control, until she touched his heated hardness, her fingers closing around him, each movement making her feel more powerful, more in control.

His hand caught her arm and she looked deep into his eyes, seeing the battle between ecstasy and control being waged there. 'We have all night, *cara.'*

She smiled and quirked a brow at him, shocked to discover the mischievous imp that lurked within her. She tried to pull her wrist free, but he held her tightly and before she could say anything had pushed her back onto the throw. Quickly and expertly he rolled on a condom then covered her body with his. She smiled impishly at him, and teased him by moving her hips, pressing herself against him. He shut his eyes and raised his head. She reached up and kissed his chest, feeling the guttural groan as well as hearing it.

'You teased me first.' She lifted her legs, wrapping them around him, the throw slipping away so she could feel the heat of the fire. The tip of his erection touched her and his body seemed gripped by rigidity, every muscle fighting against her new-found seductress.

Emboldened, she rotated her hips, sliding her hands over his back, feeling the tension there, wishing he would let go and give in to the moment, as she was. She wanted him inside her, deep inside her.

A harsh torrent of Italian, so fast she couldn't possibly understand it, rushed from him as she lifted her hips higher and took him inside her. She closed her eyes against the building fire that threatened to explode when he thrust into her. She cried out with shocked pleasure as he filled her, moving with her until their bodies became damp and their cries mingled in the darkness.

Slowly her breathing returned to normal

and he kissed her face softly, pulling her into the warmth of his body. The heat of the fire warmed her back as she lay facing him, looking into dark eyes that still smouldered with passion. She shivered as a tremor of shock slipped over her. She'd given herself to him, not just her virginity but her heart. She'd thought one night would be uncomplicated, but he'd taken a little piece of her heart.

Beyond the walls of the manor the wind wailed. 'I've never done that before,' she whispered, and moved instinctively closer to him, suddenly aware of what she'd told him. 'Been so spontaneous, I mean.'

He looked at her, desire still filling his eyes, but a hint of suspicion lingered there too. 'I know.'

She tried for bravado, desperate to hide how vulnerable she felt right now. 'No, but I guess I can tick that off my list now.'

'You should have told me you were a virgin.' He brushed his fingers along her shoulder, the expression on his face full of disbelief. 'I assumed that as you'd been engaged you would have made love before.'

Embarrassment raced over her as his fingers trailed lightly and slowly down her spine, his words unlocking the past with alarming speed. 'I guess I always pushed Jason away, determined not to be left broken-hearted, like my mother.'

He didn't say anything, didn't ask her to enlarge on it, but being so far removed from reality she couldn't stop the words flowing out. 'After my father died my mother met a new man. He made her happy but I just saw it a way of mending her heart and replacing my father.'

'Sorry.' He whispered that one word against her hair as he pulled her close, as if he was trying to chase away her demons.

Now with adult eyes she knew her mother had lost the man she'd loved with a passion. Tilly realised she too had shunned love and passion, scared of the hurt her mother had endured. She'd used the solace of the companionship and friendship she and Jason had enjoyed growing up as a protection against such emotions. She'd been too scared to love him and had denied him what he'd wanted, forcing him into the arms of another woman.

'As a child, I could never understand why she wanted to be with someone else.' It was strange how things suddenly looked so different. With just the orange glow from the fire and Xavier's arms around her she felt safe to talk, safe to explore her past. She carried on. The floodgates had been opened. 'It's been over ten years since my father died and I think part of my mother died that day too. I didn't want to be like that.'

'Do you still see your father's family?' He began to stroke her hair and at first it was soothing, but very quickly the sizzle inside her grew and she moved to look into his face.

'I haven't seen them or been back to Tuscany since my father died.' Not wanting to talk about things that hurt, she focused instead on rekindling the burning need that had claimed her, forcing her to accept she did have passion flowing in her veins. She pressed her lips against his and he responded, pulling her against his hardening body and the conclusion of the kiss was sealed.

Xavier woke in the early hours, not because of his usual nightmares but because of the warmth of Tilly's body against his. The room was darker and much colder. Carefully he moved away from Tilly and went to the fire, stoking it before putting on more logs. He watched the flames as they flickered into life, wrapping around the wood. That was what had happened to him. The flames of passion had engulfed him, not letting him go, making him want the impossible.

She'd cast a spell on him, holding him captive, but he wished she'd trusted him enough to have told him she'd been a virgin.

She murmured and he turned to look at her, but thankfully she didn't wake. As the glow from the fire began to reach the darker corners of the room, it caressed her partially uncovered body. Her golden hair was spread out around her and her face was serene and peaceful.

In an effort to ensure the fire would last as long as possible he put more logs on and made his way back to their makeshift bed.

'Xavier?' Her throaty whisper, totally unexpected, almost froze him to the spot.

'*Scusi,*' he apologised as he got back beneath the covers. 'I didn't mean to wake you.'

She gave him a sleepy smile and looked into his face as he lay next to her, his head propped on one elbow. 'How did you hurt yourself so badly?'

Her words slammed into him, instantly killing the lust that had begun to course through him once more. He didn't want to tell anyone about it, least of all Tilly and certainly not here, not in this haven from reality, where emotions he'd thought dead were being revived.

'There is nothing to tell.' He caressed her cheek with the backs of his fingers, keeping his words soft, aiming for distraction, trying to pull them back into the clutches of desire.

It almost worked. Her eyelashes fluttered closed and he relaxed just a little, then she opened those big blue eyes and looked into his, sympathy—or was that pity?—in hers. 'I've seen, Xavier, just now...'

Her words faltered to nothing as he glared at her. 'Just now what?'

'I saw the scars. It must have been a really bad accident.'

'*Sì*, it was.' He bit back the anger and guilt cocktail that rushed into his bloodstream at the memories. He could hear again the crunching of metal and the sickening thud that haunted his dreams. He could feel his body being thrown around, smashing into barriers with ferocious force. Pain had robbed him of consciousness, but when he'd come round in hospital it had been to the most dreaded news. He'd made it. Paulo hadn't. And it had been his fault.

The usual pain spiked his legs and he bit down hard against it. He was naked and exposed before her, every emotion as vulnerable and bare as his body. This was exactly the sit-

uation he'd avoided since that day in hospital
when Carlota had been so revolted by his injuries. Guilt racked him because he'd sent her
away. Frequent dates had earned him a playboy reputation, but Tilly was the first woman
he'd spent the night with since the accident.

He still didn't know if it was his battered
body or the guilt hanging over him like a storm
cloud that made him cold and uncaring. He
didn't deserve anything remotely warm like
affection and sympathy. And Tilly deserved
better.

'What are you doing?' He growled the question out, moving quickly as Tilly pulled the
throw away from his legs. There was no point
in hiding any more. She'd already seen the
marks left on him from that day, so why not
let her know it all?

'Showing you it doesn't upset me.' The firmness in her voice only irritated him further.
'There was no need for darkness, no need to
put out the candles.'

He stayed still, ice curling through him as
she looked at the livid scars on his legs, the
constant reminder that he didn't deserve happiness after he'd taken it from Paulo's family
with his selfish desire to win.

The silence stretched between them. She

was shocked. He could see it in her eyes. Damn it, she couldn't even find the words to voice her disgust, but after what she'd just given him he owed this much to her.

Slowly she knelt up and trailed her fingertips down his thigh, over the ugly and gnarled skin. He held his breath as she moved below his knee where the pins held him together.

Anger surged through him. He was no longer in control. He was now the vulnerable one. 'Those scars are nothing compared to the fact that I lived and another man died—and it was my fault.'

Her hand froze and slowly she looked at him, shock in her eyes, in the lift of her delicate brows and those soft sensual lips. The disbelieving whisper of her words told him all he needed to know. 'Your fault?'

'I wanted to win—at any cost,' he said, and scowled at the memories, wanting to shock her, punish her for seeing him like this. 'It's my fault. Paulo died because of me, because of my selfish need to be number one. I killed my friend.'

'No.' She pulled her hand away from him and sat back against the sofa, clutching one of the throws against her nakedness.

'It's not just my injuries that mean I can no

longer race. It's the guilt that another man will never be on the track again.'

She didn't say anything else, just looked at him, and he knew what they'd shared so briefly was over. Reality had already crept in.

'As you started the race, did you plan to crash?' Her tone was serious and strong.

He flung up his hands in exasperation. '*Dio mio*, of course I didn't.'

'Then it was an accident. Tragic, yes, but an accident.' She moved towards him with purpose, pity in her eyes. She reached up and touched his face, the caress too gentle, too caring.

'No.' He grabbed her wrist firmly, shock making her gasp.

He couldn't shake off the past that easily. What if she hated him after this? What if she stayed here with him simply because she didn't want to be alone in the dark and unfamiliar house?

'It's not your fault,' she whispered. 'Tonight it's as if we've stepped into another world, away from everyone and everything. Let's stay there, make the most of it and forget everything. Everything, Xavier.'

She lowered herself over him, kissing him, kissing his scars and smothering the guilt their conversation had evoked. At first he couldn't move, but fear of her rejection was gradually being replaced by hot desire. As she moved up his body to his chest, he caught her face between his hands and kissed her as if his life depended on it.

As the kiss continued, he closed his eyes against the demons from the accident, desperate to recapture the magic he and Tilly had shared just a few hours ago. Slowly her fingers trailed down his chest, tantalising and teasing, and reality slipped away.

CHAPTER EIGHT

As MORNING LIGHT filtered into the room, Tilly stretched under the warmth of the covers, her body languidly replete and her mind full of hot memories from last night. Could that woman really have been her? She'd never known such a passionate side to her existed. Neither had she ever wanted to find out—until Xavier had come into her life. He'd lit the fire of passion within her and now she didn't want it extinguished.

At that thought the smile slipped from her lips. She'd been scared to let passion enter her relationship with Jason, scared to disturb the friendship they'd had since school. It had been that reluctance that had sealed their fate. He'd never demanded anything from her, had always been the model boyfriend, but a few months before their wedding day something had changed. He'd withdrawn from her, become less interested in planning their wedding, but she'd ploughed on, desperate to stay behind the barriers of safety.

All she'd ever needed had been the safe, comfortable companionship Jason had offered ever since they'd met. Now, after what she and Xavier had experienced last night, she could begin to understand why Jason had had an affair. She only wished he hadn't left it to the last minute to tell her. She couldn't forgive him for that.

She rolled over in the improvised bed, shocked to discover she was alone. Did Xavier regret last night already? Had her passion been too much? Did he think she was looking for more than one night, even though she'd told him it was on her list? She'd had her romantic fling. It had been amazing, but she wasn't going to allow him to reject her.

She threw back the throw, the chilled air making her skin prickle and she looked around for her clothes, embarrassment flooding her as she remembered the brazen way she'd discarded them and the hungry way she'd watched Xavier do the same. Quickly she grabbed her bra and jumper and shivered as she put them on.

She remembered the way he'd flinched and watched her as she'd touched his scarred legs and waist. He'd helped her get over the past, even though he didn't know it, and she'd wanted to help him too, by proving the scars didn't matter. But from the way he'd made love to her afterwards, without the gentleness of the first time, she knew she'd only angered him.

Just as she'd finished pulling on her crumpled clothes, Xavier returned, looking fierce, his dark eyes holding her captive.

'Going somewhere?' The harshness of his tone sent a chill that was colder than the snow outside down her spine. He was still angry. The intensely sexy man from last night had gone.

'To see if it has stopped snowing.' She said the first thing that came to mind, unsure what she had been planning on doing next.

He glared at her. Did he regret that not only had he spent the night with his hired help, he'd bared his soul, told her his inner most thoughts? She'd seen the scarring on his legs, something she guessed he didn't allow many women to see, and her heart had constricted. It had stirred her passion, turning it into something far more intense, and all she'd wanted to do was love him.

A tingle of alarm rushed over her as she realised she'd done the one thing she'd always avoided. She'd lost control of her emotions. But did she love him? No, she'd only wanted a fling, but hadn't she already admitted to herself he'd taken a bit of her heart?

The questions continued to rush around her mind. She pretended to be busy folding the throws, desperate not to look at his icy-cold expression. Love didn't happen that fast, she had merely been consumed by what she'd striven to avoid all her adult life. Passion—the emotion linked to pain and loneliness.

Her mother was proof that neither love nor passion could save a person from heartache. Why would anyone want something so destructive? Even as the thought entered her mind, she knew why. The intense passion of loving that she'd discovered last night was the reason and she shut those thoughts away. Her fling was over. Time to get back to reality.

She thought of the hours she and Xavier had spent making love. Her body could still feel every caress, every kiss and every hot spark of desire. But now despair filled her heart. It hadn't helped her to move on, as she'd foolishly believed. It had only made things worse.

'Let's hope we can escape this place today.' Xavier all but growled the words out. He was putting distance between them. She got the message loud and clear. Last night was well and truly over.

It's for the best, she told herself as she walked to the window to see if escape, as he'd called it, was possible. One thing was for sure, she had no intention of hanging around for his rejection. He'd turned his girlfriend away, so pushing her away would be easy. She'd been rejected by Jason and she certainly wasn't going to meekly wait for it to happen again. This time she would do the rejecting.

Feeling suffocated and hemmed in, she roughly pulled open the curtains, her agitation showing in every movement until she froze. She couldn't believe what she was seeing. It was still snowing. The possibility of leaving today didn't look good. 'No, it can't be,' she whispered, more to herself than to the man whose brooding presence filled the room.

Behind her she heard the flick of the light switch and turned to face him. 'The power is still out.' His eyes, cold and dark, met hers.

Could this get any worse? She'd just spent the night with the man who was effectively her boss, shared secrets they both probably would never have told, and now they were going to be forced to spend yet another day alone in the same house.

'It's still snowing.' Her voice was barely above a whisper as she tried to take in what this all meant.

She turned to face him, wanting to prove to herself she was in control, that she wouldn't dissolve into a distressed heap in front of him. Right now she didn't care what he thought of her. All she cared about was dousing the passion once and for all. It couldn't happen again.

'So, we are completely cut off. Snowbound.' His sharp tone caught her unawares and she couldn't think what to do now, her mind in a panic.

'I need to leave today. I have to go.'

She had to get to Vanessa's, but, more importantly, she had to get away from Xavier.

Xavier marched to the window and looked out at the white landscape. Snow was plastered to the sides of trees and bushes as if someone had painted them with a brush. They could be stuck here for several days.

How were they going to move on from their conversation in the early hours of this morning? He'd opened up to her, believing they would be parting the next morning. He couldn't spend the day with her after that revelation. What if they were stuck here? What would happen tonight?

He remembered every detail of last night as the blizzard had done its worst outside. Her total innocence and how he'd let her into his mind. But as dawn had broken, reality had begun to creep back stealthily.

'We should have tried to go yesterday.' She dragged her hands through her hair and instantly he recalled how his fingers had slid through its thickness last night.

Enough, he berated himself. It had been exactly that sort of emotion that had lowered his defences, allowed her to touch his heart. The heart he'd kept frozen for the last three years.

He looked at her face, at the horror of their situation reflected in her eyes. He knew she thought he was blaming her. But he wasn't. He'd messed up enough lives with the accident and now he was messing up hers, opening up wounds he'd never known she'd nursed, wounds as big as those he was trying to heal.

'It's not going to help to stand here, apportioning blame. After breakfast I will walk to the road to see what the situation is.' He was back in charge, back in control, which was more than he'd been last night.

'I'm coming too.' The firm statement left him in no doubt that she intended to do just that. 'I've seen more boots and coats in one of the back rooms.'

Va bene. He could see any kind of refusal

was useless. Thankfully, minute by minute, he was regaining control, not only of his emotions but the situation.

The strong, hot coffee, brewed on the gas stove, had further infused him with discipline, so that by the time they were making their way through the deep snow he was in a more amenable mood.

Just as when she'd arrived, Tilly wore her red woollen hat and scarf. Her cheeks were flushed from the freezing wind and a worried look haunted her eyes. Was it really that important to get to her friend's house? A real friend would understand. These thoughts cluttered his mind, filling it with questions, until Tilly stumbled into a windblown patch of snow, which was far deeper than she'd expected, and with a squeal of shock she flung out her arms.

He caught her instantly, his reactions quick and precise. But instead of letting her go as soon as she was steady on her feet, he held her close. She looked up at him, wide-eyed, and that strange sensation filled his chest, squashing almost all the breath from him. Despite their bundled layers he could feel the heat from her body infusing his and the urge to kiss her was so strong he had to grit his teeth against it.

Again she was testing him. *Dio mio.* What had she done to him?

He'd pushed her boundaries, knocked them down, all for his own selfish needs, had divulged all his secrets, but he still wanted her.

'We should continue,' he managed to say over the thrum of lust. 'The sky is looking more threatening, as if more snow is on the way.'

'So much snow.' Tilly couldn't believe it. More snow meant not only being unable to get to Vanessa's but also being here longer with Xavier. That was something she couldn't do, especially when he looked at her with such intolerance in his eyes. He didn't want to be here with her, much less be reminded of the mistake they'd made last night.

Their passion had been all-consuming, totally undeniable. She'd always thought passion caused trouble, that unhappiness was just a kiss away—and it had certainly proved to be true. One kiss had led to last night and now he could barely look at her.

'We will see what the lanes look like then decide what to do.' The command in his voice was strong, adding weight to her theory that he now despised her. She'd pushed him to talk, forced him to reveal not just his scars but his feelings. He was shutting himself away, becoming unreachable.

She pulled away from him, away from the burning anger that sparked so vibrantly in his eyes. 'Even if the lanes are clear, I'll never get the van out of here.'

Despair flooded through her. Her mind was so full of anxiety she wanted to drop to the snow and give up, but that would be showing weakness and you never let your enemy see that. He may well have been her lover for just those few short hours, but the way he was treating her now he was as good as her enemy.

'Maybe not, but we could try and get you to the main road and public transport.'

So he was that desperate to be rid of her and the problem created by last night's passionate encounter that he would pack her up and put her on a bus.

'It's snowing, Xavier. Buses will not be running. Not today.' The spark of fire in her voice shocked her and, judging by the way he looked at her, it had shocked him too. Those coolly assessing eyes held hers and for a moment everything was silent, muffled by the snow and the tension stretching between them.

'Come.' The command in his voice was strong and clear, but he held out his hand to her. She looked at it, knowing taking hold of it would change everything. 'Natalie?'

She took his hand, not knowing why or what she hoped would happen, but she hadn't anticipated the zing of electricity that zipped up her arm.

'I don't like this.' She'd spoken before she could think. 'Being stuck here, I mean.'

'Because of the snow or me?' He fired the question at her as he strode through the deep snow. Finally they reached the part of the driveway that twisted through the woods and where the depth of snow was less, sheltered by the trees.

'Both,' she answered honestly.

They'd reached the small bridge, the stream below, iced at the edges, leaving just a trickle of moving water. He pulled her to a stop, forcing her to face him, but didn't let go of her hand.

'What happened last night…' he began, but she cut him off.

'No, not now.' She didn't want to hear his admission that he'd never meant it to happen, that he'd never intended to make love to her with such passion, because that would be too painful. Last night should have been about just one night. A fling. But she'd let passion rule and with a start she realised she had fallen in love with him.

She had no idea how it had happened, how her feelings had turned to something so powerful, but they had. Now she had to block that out, stop the surge of love that had flowed through her. And she would.

'Yes, now, Natalie.' He touched his free hand to her cold face, shocking her into looking at him. 'Last night needs to be discussed—right now.'

'No, it doesn't. It happened. That's all we need to say.' She pulled herself free and walked away as best she could through the snow. The shrill call of a blackbird startled by her sudden movement made her falter and he caught hold of her again.

'Don't walk away from me, Natalie.' The gruff harshness of his voice shocked her as it seemed to echo in the snow-covered branches above them.

'It doesn't matter if I stand here or walk away, Xavier. Nothing will change what happened. There is nothing we can say that will change that.'

'Or the fact that it shouldn't have happened?' At first she thought he was stating a fact, but the inflection of those last words changed it to a question. Or was that just his accent?

She looked at him, all the fight that had bubbled up inside her evaporating, but he was right. Question or statement, last night should never have happened. Just as she should never have kissed him on New Year's Eve, they should not have spent last night like lovers. They weren't lovers and never could be.

'Last night was a one-off, Xavier. A fling,' she said firmly, looking directly into his eyes, her strength returning with every breath she took. She'd been scared and had sought comfort in his arms, but had found so much more. She shouldn't have let her romantic fantasy carry her away, sweeping to one side her ability to think rationally.

Xavier looked down into her face, watched as the nervous hesitation in her eyes turned to sparks of determination. There were things about last night he regretted, like the fact he'd revealed far too much about himself, but not for one moment did he wish they hadn't enjoyed the passion that had flowed between them. He didn't regret making love to her, making her his.

'A night with a beautiful woman in my arms is not something I am prepared to apologise for, but I can see you would rather it hadn't happened.'

'We were seduced by the moment,' she said quickly, barely acknowledging his last words. 'Can you honestly say that if we had met at a party in London, we would have spent the night together?'

The reality of those words weren't lost on him. The fact that they were true didn't help. It would never have happened.

'I used you...used last night,' she continued boldly. 'I was proving to myself I could move on and now I know I can.'

He let her go, moved away from her, the temptation to kiss her, to taste her lips beneath his just one last time snatched away by her revelation.

'Then we both got what we wanted.' The roughness of his words shocked him.

He hadn't been seduced by the moment, he'd been seduced by her, by her kiss on New Year's Eve, which had been more than just a kiss. It had held the definite promise of more, much more. But there had been something else too, something new, something he'd never felt before, and it had stirred emotions he'd thought dead.

For the first time he'd caught a glimpse of a

happy future. He'd seen it, tasted it. It would never be possible, not now she'd made it obvious she didn't want him, that he'd been a chance opportunity to chase away the memory of another man.

If any other woman had told him that, he'd have been relieved, but hearing Tilly say it cut painfully into his slumbering emotions. It didn't alter the way he felt about her. If he didn't know better, he'd even go as far as to say it might be close to deeper feelings, the sort he'd vowed not to allow into his life because of his guilt over Paulo's death.

But Tilly didn't want him. She'd only wanted one night. He'd had the tables turned on him. He pushed the uncomfortable thought aside. There were far more important things to worry about—like getting back to London and away from Tilly.

The gates he'd driven through two days ago still stood open, snow banked up against the wrought-iron bars. The lane that wound through the trees they'd just walked under was hidden from view beneath a blanket of fluffy white snow several inches deep. Only two sets of footprints disturbed the untouched surface of whiteness. He strode past the gate and out to the road, which was equally unrecognisable. They would not be going anywhere soon, that much was evident.

He turned to look at Tilly as she stopped next to him, the look of utter devastation on her face spiking his already guilt-ridden conscience. *Dio mio*, as if he didn't already have enough guilt to carry around.

'So much for leaving today.' Her delicate brows rose sharply in a gesture of haughtiness he hadn't seen in her before.

'Sarcasm doesn't become you, Natalie.' He turned his back on the snow-covered road and looked down at her. As she glared up at him, her lips pressed into a firm and angry line, he had to fight the urge to kiss them just once more, until they became as soft and kissable as they'd been last night.

'Tilly,' she snapped at him. 'Nobody calls me Natalie now.'

'Is that what your fiancé called you?' he goaded her, and could almost see the snow melting beneath her feet as her anger simmered over and towards the boiling point.

She shook her head and sadness crept into her eyes, spiking him with another layer of guilt.

'Nonna.' Her blue eyes were glacially sharp as she looked at him and he knew he'd unexpectedly touched a raw nerve, that she was thinking about the grandmother she must have adored as a child.

'I'm sorry,' he said, moving towards her, remembering their brief conversation about her family. 'Maybe one day you will see her again.'

She shook her head vehemently. 'She passed away a few years ago. My mother and I didn't have contact with any other family in Italy. It's in the past and the past can't be changed.'

Just as last night can't be changed. The words drifted casually through his mind. Would he change it? He wouldn't change a thing since the moment she'd arrived at Wimble Manor—except her cold rejection this morning.

'I, more than most, know that is true.' He thought of all the times he'd wished he could have gone back and changed things, but no amount of wishing would bring Paulo back. Nothing could change that day, erase it from his memory, where it was branded for evermore. 'But sometimes, *cara*, you can shape the future to mend the past.'

His philosophical words taunted him cruelly. He hadn't achieved that miracle yet.

'If that is true, then we need to use last night's mistake. You and I both know it would never have happened under normal circumstances, but it did. If I believed in fate, I'd say we were meant to be here like this to heal our pain.' She looked from him to the snow-covered lane, desolation clear on her face. When she looked back at him everything about her was cool and collected, as cold as the snowy landscape.

'Is that what you really think?' He'd asked the question before he'd been able to halt the words. What had happened last night, those desire-filled hours together in front of the fire, had been so wildly passionate, so intense and new. Deep down he didn't want to turn his back on it. He'd sampled something he might never know again and a part of him couldn't let that go.

Despite her strong, almost flippant attitude this morning, her sharp words and obvious disappointment at not being able to leave, she too wanted more. She might be hiding behind the taunting admission of wanting a fling, but she couldn't ignore what drew them together—just as he couldn't.

'No.' She looked at him then began the long walk back to the manor house, forcing him to follow. 'We were just in the wrong place at the wrong time.'

CHAPTER NINE

TILLY STAMPED THE snow from her boots as she opened the back door of the manor house, grateful to be out of the cold wind. Xavier hadn't spoken since they'd turned back from the gates, but his presence next to her had been dark and brooding. He hadn't denied last night had been a mistake, or that it would never have happened if his plans hadn't been changed.

It went against everything she believed in, but she still wanted him, still hungered to explore the passion that simmered, waiting for a touch or a kiss to spark it back into life. She'd given away a piece of her heart—exactly what she'd never wanted to do.

'I have work to do this afternoon.' His heavy accent gave away the fact that he was not as in control as he wanted her to think. She'd learnt that much about him. 'I also need to find out when the power is likely to come back and if there is any way we can get out of here today.'

He definitely didn't want to be with her any longer. Last night had been enough. She'd started to tell him she wanted him, that she believed they were meant to be here, but his frozen expression told her he didn't share that view.

'Do you think that's possible?' She couldn't stay here. How could she ever have thought a fling with Xavier would help her?

He shrugged out of his coat, hung it up and looked down at her. 'Maybe not today, tomorrow perhaps.'

The sooner they returned to reality the better. 'I hope you are right.' She didn't want to be around when he tired of her, but maybe he already had.

His eyes searched hers, and for a moment she thought he might kiss her and her lips parted as her heart rate accelerated wildly. She wanted his lips on hers, wanted to be in his arms, but she couldn't be the one to start it.

'I'll make something for lunch,' she said briskly restraining her wayward desires. Her arm brushed against his as she passed him, sending a hot spark of shock through her. She had to get away from him. Maybe then she could rationalise what was happening between them. Label it and shut it away, never to be explored again. It had happened and evidently he wished it hadn't.

With this thought in mind Tilly made herself scarce all afternoon, spending time wandering around the rest of the old house, but it was too cold to linger for long and as the afternoon began to fade she made her way to the small lounge they'd slept in last night, anxious that the electricity still wasn't working. The thought of spending the night alone in the cold darkness of her room was like being abandoned all over again, but she couldn't let it show.

'Looks like we still need the candles,' she said casually as she entered the room, to find Xavier sitting at his desk, with one candle alight and the fire burning brightly, reminding her of last night all over again.

She felt him look at her but moved to the window and stared out at the snowy landscape. It had stopped snowing, the wind had calmed and the first few stars were beginning to show themselves in the twilight sky.

He dropped his pen onto the desk, the noise making her turn to him. 'Don't worry, *cara*, I have made enquiries this afternoon. We should have the power back by nightfall.'

Relief flooded her, quickly followed by regret. She wouldn't have to worry about the darkness tonight, but that also meant she would have to sleep alone and after last night that was going to be hard, especially when they were still in their surreal world, still very much alone. The thought of continuing her romantic fling filtered through, but that would never happen. It had just been one night to him and should have been the same for her, but it wasn't.

'That's a relief,' she said quickly, trying to hide the blush that crept over her cheeks just thinking of what had happened in this very room last night. She had to remember Xavier Moretti could never be part of her life.

'So you don't like the idea of another night in front of the fire?' The teasing torment in his voice was hard to ignore as he unwittingly tapped into her thoughts. She continued to stare out at the wintery scene, knowing he was watching her. She could feel his eyes on her, knew by her racing pulse that it was more than a curious glance. 'That is not very spontaneous.'

She whirled round to face him. She'd never

been like that, preferring always to be in control. That way she didn't risk being hurt. It was why she didn't understand the way she acted around Xavier. No man had ever made her so reckless, but, then, never before had she intended to have a fling. 'No, it's not, and as we've established, last night should not have happened.'

'You were very spontaneous last night—and very passionate.'

He stopped in mid-sentence and she walked towards him, eager to make her point but instantly wishing she hadn't as her body leapt to life with heat and desire. 'Last night I wasn't myself. I have never done anything like that before.'

'I understand, Tilly.' The smooth seductiveness of his voice caressed her jangled nerves, soothing the anxiety. 'Much more than you might think.'

As if sensing she was giving in, he stood up and very slowly moved towards her. 'What do you understand?' The question came out as a whisper as she tried to think over the throbbing beat of her pulse. How could this be happening again? How could she lose control of herself so quickly?

'That you were afraid of the passion that

burnt in you, afraid because of what happened with Jason.'

'It has nothing to do with Jason.' As she spoke, everything became clear. She'd loved Jason in a gentle, platonic kind of way and it had taken Xavier and one enforced night in his company to show her what real love was.

No wonder Jason had wanted more than companionship. She hadn't been able to love or let passion into her heart and their relationship. Her childhood had ensured that but it didn't justify him jilting her on their wedding day.

She looked at Xavier, the man she had been passionate with, and saw the dark intensity in his eyes. Did he believe her? Did he know he'd unlocked things she'd been shutting out all her adult life?

'Well, *mia cara*, whatever the reason for last night, you should be that spontaneous woman again, live for the moment, but most of all you should let passion into your life.'

'Is that the voice of experience?' She couldn't keep the mocking tone from her voice. Who was he to tell her what she should be?

He moved closer still but she didn't step back, even though she could have. She held his gaze, desperate to prove passion wasn't burning inside her, as he'd said. But it was a lie. The embers of last night were being coaxed to life. It was happening all over again and she couldn't let it.

Suddenly the dimly lit room was flooded with light. Lamps glowed as the power returned. The shadows receded, taking with them her fears and the passion Xavier had almost rekindled.

'Thank goodness.' Quickly she moved away from him and the temptation of his touch. 'At least we will have heat and light this evening.' It also meant she'd be able to sleep alone in her bed.

'And we will not have to spend another night here in front of the fire?' His sexy accent gave those words a deeper meaning, one she couldn't think about.

She shot him a glance, his dry tone echoing her own relief. She had to get out of here right now, before she gave in to the newly discovered spontaneity he'd mentioned and asked him to take her to his bed.

'As you are busy with work, I will say goodnight.' She kept her voice firm and devoid of any emotion, the unruffled exterior she normally lived behind returning as the panic of earlier ebbed away.

His brows flicked up briefly, but the shocked expression was soon replaced by the cold calmness she'd seen that morning. 'That is not necessary, not when there is a warm fire here.'

'I think it is, Xavier. As I said earlier, what happened last night shouldn't have.'

'But it did happen, *cara*.' He moved towards her again. She held her ground, standing tall, her chin lifted in a blatant show of defiance. 'And that cannot be undone.'

'I know that.' The strangled whisper that slipped from her alarmed her as much as the thought of spending more time with a man who made her feel emotions she just wasn't ready to experience.

'Take candles and matches with you,' he said dismissively, and even though she was relieved he'd let the subject go, she couldn't help the disappointment that crashed over her.

'Goodnight, Xavier.' She forced as much control as possible into her voice, picked up the candles and matches and headed for the door. She was almost sorry to leave the warmth of the fire for a room that would probably still be cold after almost twenty-four hours without heat, but she couldn't stay here with him any longer. Not when he tested her, pushing

her towards everything she'd always resisted—
everything she should still resist.

'Tilly?'

'Yes?' She swung round to look at him,
cursing the excited hope that flared to life.

'Sleep well.'

She nodded then left before she gave in to
the temptation to rush over to him, throw her
arms around him and be the woman she'd been
last night—the woman who loved him.

Xavier watched Tilly go and felt every last bit
of willpower being tested. He wanted to go
after her, sweep her into his arms and carry
her to the large four-poster bed in which he'd
spent the first night at the manor—alone.

He wanted to kiss her until she surrendered
to him. He wanted to lure out the woman he
knew deep down she was. The passionate and
sexy woman who'd spent last night in his arms.

Instead he stayed brooding over his paperwork, her claims that last night had been a mistake banging around in his head. Obviously,
despite her bold way of proving his scars didn't
matter and telling him the accident had been
just that, she felt differently.

She was the only woman he'd let close since
the accident, the only woman he'd made love

to—and she was pushing him away, telling him a fling was all she'd wanted. Yet she'd been a virgin.

Maybe it was just as well the electricity was back on. It would stop him making the same mistake twice and prevent his life becoming complicated. He wasn't ready for a relationship. With those thoughts, he went to his room, intending to take a cold shower and get some sleep, but as he stood, towel around his hips, looking at his reflection in the bathroom mirror after shaving, he questioned if sleep would be possible.

How could he sleep alone after last night, when the woman who'd allowed him to take something so precious, who'd shown him things he could never have, filling the night with compassion as well as hot desire, was only a few rooms away? She was that close, but so very far out of reach.

A fluid Italian curse left his lips and he flung the towel to the bathroom floor, as if it was responsible for the wild rush of emotions coursing through him. Damn it, he wanted her, he wanted the happy future she'd allowed him to glimpse, the one she'd had snatched from her.

But she doesn't want you. Dio mio! What was wrong with him? Since when did he believe in relationships and happiness? He'd destroyed Paulo's family and deserved to be punished over and over. Love and happiness could never reach him through his barrier of guilt—or so he'd thought.

He got into bed and switched out the light, the darkness wrapping around him instantly. He thought of Tilly, lying alone in her bed, and wanted nothing more than to go to her and hold her, but even more he wanted to love her. Could she have changed him that much in one night?

With a growl of exasperation he threw back the covers, flicked on the bedside lamp and pulled on his jeans. He couldn't ignore what burned inside him for the blonde who'd exploded into his life such a short time ago and had inexplicably become a part of it.

His bare feet were silent on the carpeted landing as he made his way to the top of the stairs. In the dim light he could see the Christmas tree. It still mocked him, still reminded him he didn't deserve Christmas and the happiness it brought.

Did that mean he didn't deserve Tilly and the happiness he'd begun to imagine with her?

Should he stop and return to his room? No, he couldn't turn his back on not only Tilly but the happiness she would bring to his life. He paused at the top of the stairs and looked down the corridor that led to Tilly's room.

They were still snowed in, still away from the harsh reality of the real world, and that changed things. Was one more night in that surreal world possible?

He turned away. She deserved better than him and so much more than he could give. She deserved happiness *and* love. With heaviness settling over him, he walked away, turning his back on what could have been if he hadn't been the man he was.

Tilly hadn't slept at all and without knowing why had slipped out of bed and from her room. Where was Xavier now? Was he alone downstairs, punishing himself? She wished she could make him see he shouldn't, make him see he deserved to be loved and had to let love back into his life.

She stopped briefly in the darkened corridor, nervous of the shadows lurking in the old house, but the need to go to Xavier, to be with him, to love him—for just one more night— was too much. She made her way along the corridor to the top of the stairs. It wasn't just the passion and desire that had turned her whole world upside down last night that drove her on in this madness. It was the love for him, growing deep inside her. This was far more than being spontaneous.

She wanted to show him her love, just one more time, because tomorrow, however it was accomplished, she was leaving. She had to get back to her life. The one without love and passion complicating it, but tonight she wanted to live the fantasy one last time. She wouldn't be leading him on, not when he preferred affairs to relationships. She would just blur into one of many who'd warmed his bed. That thought didn't sit comfortably, but her need for him was far stronger and she wanted to take the risk that being with him most definitely was.

Nothing else mattered. She had to go to him—just one last time.

As she came to the landing and the top of the elegant staircase she saw him. Like a vision conjured up from her dreams, dressed only in his jeans, the look on his face so distant. Traces of vulnerability lingered in his eyes and she could hardly believe it was the same man she'd said goodnight to earlier.

'Tilly?' The question lingered in the syllables of her name.

She took a deep breath. Now was a time

to be bold. 'I want to be someone different, Xavier, to live in a world of complete fantasy and be the woman I was last night—just once more.'

Before she had a chance to register his re-action, he'd come to her, his fingers brushing down her face as he stood half-naked in front of her. Her pulse leapt and she looked up into his dark eyes, wondering if he felt it too, this passion that had taken her over. It was so intense she trembled like a leaf in the summer breeze.

'You are tempting me so much I can't resist.' His voice held a faint tremor, as if he did feel it.

He lowered his head and brushed his lips lightly over hers and she closed her eyes as pleasure swept away any lingering doubts about what she was doing. Her body leaned towards him, but he didn't take her in his arms, didn't pull her against his body.

She opened her eyes and looked into the fathomless depths of his. They had only one more night left in this strange world where rules and barriers were being eroded. 'Xavier?'

'Shhh. Forget the world exists, just for to-night.' His breath whispered across her lips and she knew it was too late, she was already his.

'Yes,' she whispered, and then pressed her lips to his briefly. 'Just for tonight.'

Somewhere deep inside her she was screaming—no, shouting—that one night would never be enough, not now she'd fallen in love with him, but sense prevailed. She knew not to expect any kind of commitment from him.

As doubts rose again he kissed her passionately, pulling her against his bare chest, making further thought impossible as the desire they'd shared the previous night erupted once more. Then he swept her up in his arms and made his way to his bedroom. She could feel each stride taking her past the point of no return, but she didn't care. All she wanted was to love him, one last time.

CHAPTER TEN

XAVIER WOKE WITH a start, his bare shoulders cold, but the warmth of Tilly's body curled against his was a stark reminder of what had happened last night. Once again they'd spent the night in each other's arms.

He'd experienced how loving could be and had wanted to be loved by her, and not just physically. But Tilly had made it clear it was only one more night, the last time before they returned to their normal lives. This was just a fling to her.

He reminded himself again that he didn't deserve anything remotely like love. Not when he'd broken a family apart as easily as his bike had smashed. He dragged his thoughts back to Tilly. Had she been sent to punish him?

She'd been distant as she'd left the lounge last night and he still didn't understand what had compelled him to go to her room. He'd known it was wrong to want her and he'd turned away, remembering how she'd told him the previous night had been a mistake. But there had been moments today when she couldn't deny what had exploded to life between them. Or was it merely her damn list?

He'd wanted her again but had turned back, accepting if she had wanted to be with him she wouldn't have made her excuses and gone so early to her room. But at the top of the stairs he'd sensed her, had felt her gaze on him. She too must have been drawn by the same need. Although this time he'd had no darkness to conceal how underserving of such a moment he was. But it hadn't mattered.

He relaxed a little, the curtains at the corner of the big four-poster bed partially cocooning them, and he watched her sleep, felt every breath she took and inhaled the scent that was uniquely Tilly. Her claims of yesterday morning burned into his mind. He had been nothing more than a challenge to banish demons from her past, to rid herself of Jason. Had last night been to make sure she had achieved that?

He moved away from her, the soft sigh as she stirred making him drag in a deep breath against the rise of desire. Whatever her reaction was going to be when she woke up, he didn't want to deal with it—not yet. He needed to steel himself against the moment she would turn her back on him.

It was only a matter of time before the passion they'd shared for a second night was obliterated by the harshness of daylight, just as it had been yesterday. He had to send her away. He had to end it, whatever it was.

He unwound himself from her warm body and got out of bed, pulled on his clothes and slipped from the room. He didn't trust himself to glance back at the woman asleep in his bed. He couldn't. Everything was becoming far too complicated. It had been more than a lust-filled night. He'd never wanted to feel anything more than basic desire for her. Yet she'd crept under his defences, giving him hope that maybe he did deserve to love, that he could put everything behind him.

But that wasn't enough for him. She'd seen beyond the scars on his legs but would she see past his guilt? His actions on the track had killed Paulo—his friend. If *he* couldn't forgive himself, nobody else would.

He glared at the Christmas tree as he went down the stairs, muttering curses beneath his breath. Had the damn thing cursed him? No, he'd done that all by himself.

He marched into the small lounge and glanced out of the window. Thankfully it hadn't snowed again. At least he could organise to get them away from here. He picked up his phone from the desk and as he turned he saw the fire, now just a mass of grey cold ashes. It had been as hot as the passion between him and Tilly when they'd spent the night beneath throws in front of it.

He cursed fluidly in Italian. He and Tilly could never be together. She was far better off without him in her life. He was being selfish to want her. For once in his life he'd think of someone else. It was, after all, just a fling to get over another man she'd wanted.

Angered by that thought, he quickly accessed his emails, sending a message first to Paulo's widow, warning her he might not make it to her charity event in Milan, then to a friend in London, explaining the situation and asking if they could source a car and driver who could cope in the conditions as quickly as possible, stressing it had to be today. He pressed 'send' but it didn't make him feel relieved at all. It only highlighted that he couldn't spend another night with Tilly, although he wanted many more nights such as last night.

'Morning.' Tilly's voice broke into his

thoughts as she walked into the room, dressed once more in her jeans and black roll neck jumper. 'Thank goodness it didn't snow any more in the night. Maybe we can leave today.'

'Buon giorno.' Part of him wished it had snowed, wished that it was so deep they'd be here for days, locking them away from the world and reality in a place where they could explore the desire that raged between them. 'I've made enquiries about someone fetching us today.'

Their eyes met and in those few seconds he thought he saw sadness in hers, but then it was gone. 'Good,' she said with obvious relief, walking to the window, looking out as the rising sun cast an orange glow on everything. 'It looks so pretty out there, but it must be cold.'

'Freezing.' He joined her at the window, resisting the urge to stand too close. If he did, he'd want to take her in his arms and kiss her. Such thoughts had to be pushed firmly from his mind, for her sake. Their time together was almost over. The real world called.

Tilly stood by the window, looking out at the snow, desperately trying not to notice the way her heart leapt just because Xavier had moved closer. Again he'd left her as daylight had returned. Alone in his bed, the bed he'd carried her to. It had given a clear message, just as she had when they'd met on the landing. By leaving her this morning he was saying it was over, which made it easier, because if he'd kissed her again…

As he stood looking out at the snow he didn't make any reference to last night. Despite what she'd told him, part of her hoped that at least he would acknowledge their night together. If that didn't tell her it was over, nothing did, but the sense of loss which filled her was intense.

By this evening she would be back in her flat. All she wanted now was to leave this place and go back to her life as if their paths had never crossed, although her bucket list would be one item shorter.

She turned away from the window, the cold and lifeless hearth of the fire signifying her moment out of reality was over. She didn't know how long she could keep up the pretence of indifference when every nerve in her body was screaming for him.

'When do you expect someone to arrive?' She all but snapped the words at him in an attempt to stay in control of her battered emotions.

'It will be at least lunchtime, but we should

be back in London by the evening.' He strode across the room and stood by the open door. She looked up at him, seeing not a trace of the man she'd spent the last two days with. 'I'll make us some breakfast.'

'No, I should do that.' If he made her breakfast after what they'd shared last night, it would be too intimate and too painful.

'No, you are my guest.' The insistence in his voice halted her, stemming the flow of anxious words from bubbling up within her. She'd been his guest since midnight on New Year's Eve and had become just another woman on his long list of conquests, exactly what she hadn't wanted to be.

Before she could argue further he left and for a moment she just stood staring at where he'd been standing. Inside her something snapped, or fell into place. Either way, things had changed. 'Do you always make women breakfast?'

'Never.' He marched off, his icy comment lingering in the air as if winter had entered the house.

She was just one of many who'd shared his bed, his passion, but never his love. For the last two nights she'd loved him, not just with her body but with her heart. She'd known it was a mistake. He'd slipped beneath the barricades she'd put up around her heart, determined to keep out such emotions. Now he would break her heart, saying goodbye. But he wasn't her Mr Right, not a womanising man like Xavier Moretti, and she'd do well to remember that.

'At least let me help.' From deep within her she drew on strength and courage she hadn't known she had. He would never know just what he'd unlocked.

He looked at her, raising a brow in that devilishly handsome way, sending her pulse racing. 'I think I'm capable of making breakfast so, please, sit and relax.'

He glanced at her when she sat at the kitchen table. It all felt too real, too much like normal life and not at all like the nights they had shared. Once again daylight was bringing harsh reality. How could he act as if it hadn't happened?

'I know your *nonna* gave you a love of food and cooking, but what made you set up a business?' He stopped what he was doing and looked at her, directly into her eyes, his dark ones searching hers. But what for? What was he hoping to find?

She held his gaze boldly. Did he know he'd touched a raw nerve, hit on the one thing she didn't want to talk about, this morning of all mornings? The last three days had made her look at everything differently, from her need to stay professional to the realisation that she'd never loved Jason, not passionately. She'd also questioned the inability to contact her father's family, knowing it was because she feared their rejection. They'd done it to her mother, only Nonna having maintained contact.

'I guess I was looking for a challenge and a bit of spontaneity in my life.' She used his advice from last night, turned it around and made it fit her explanation, hoping that would be the end of the discussion.

'As good a reason as any,' he said, and cracked eggs into a bowl, whisking them with obvious ease. Everything seemed so relaxed—apart from her.

'I'm impressed.' She couldn't help but tease him. He really did bring out the lighter side of her, the side that didn't worry and question everything, not needing to always be in total control. He'd coaxed out her spontaneous side a bit further with each falling snowflake.

'Then my first mission of the day is complete.' He put the eggs and toast on the table and sat down, his handsome face holding a hint of mischief. He was enjoying this.

'And your second mission? Is that to get back to London?' The questions slipped from her before she thought of any consequences, and judging by the look he cast her way it was exactly what he was hoping for and she hid her desire for things to be different behind bravado. 'It will be a relief to get back to London.'

'Have you not enjoyed your time here?'

How could he ask that? Tilly's heart broke a little as the answer came to mind. Their time together had been nothing more than a fling for him. She'd been a convenient distraction from the situation they'd found themselves in and his obvious dislike of Christmas, which she knew was linked to the accident.

It should have been the same for her. Hadn't she eventually decided he was her bucket list affair? The one that would help her move on from Jason? Somewhere along the way she'd lost sight of that. Each kiss had touched her heart a little deeper, each touch binding her to him a little bit more. She hadn't wanted love, hadn't been seeking it, not after what had happened last year, but it had found her.

She looked across the table at him, trying to remember what he'd just asked her, but her mind was blank. All she could think of was that this man was the man she loved, that he could be her Mr Right if things had been different, but she could never tell him. He'd made it plain that their time together meant nothing. Thank goodness she'd told him about her list, that he was merely a tick on that list.

'I'm sorry if it's been miserable, stuck here with me.' There was a hint of hurt in his voice as he spoke firmly, bringing her rapidly from her thoughts.

'No, it's not that.' She struggled to find the right way to explain. 'Neither of us planned this to happen and if we are totally honest, we know what did happen wouldn't have if it hadn't been for the snow.'

'You are right. It wouldn't have.' The hard words fired back at her and her heart squeezed with pain. What they'd shared had been nothing more than a passing moment. Two vulnerable people stranded together, sharing secrets. But even so she'd harboured a little bit of hope.

'And once we are back in London?' She almost didn't dare ask, but she needed to know, needed to hear it from him.

For a moment she dared to allow herself to imagine him saying he wanted to see her again, that he wanted much more than just the three nights they'd spent here together. She looked at his hard expression, realising such hope was futile. What they'd shared was over. The mutually beneficial fling had come to an end, expired, just as her contract had done.

'I will have your van returned to you as soon as possible.' His voice shattered the fragile image of things she shouldn't want. The fact that *it* would be returned and not that he would return it didn't go unnoticed. All connections would be severed and his life would go on as before. Whereas hers... How could she go back to her life when he'd woken the spontaneous, happy and passionate woman she'd always wished she could be?

'I don't want anyone to know about us.' She looked down at the breakfast, which suddenly looked very unappetising. She was acting from self-preservation. There was no way she could admit what she really wanted. This was worse than her wedding morning when Jason had told her it was over. 'From a professional point of view, I don't want to risk future clients finding out.'

'*Sì*, that is best. What happened here will stay here, within these walls, probably adding to secrets from generations ago.'

She looked up at him, pain crushing her. How had she got so close so quickly? Was it simply because of the intimate moments they'd shared, the secrets they'd spoken of?

It was much more than that—for her at least. It was love. She hadn't ever allowed herself to fall in love, not even with Jason, and without realising it she'd fallen in love with Xavier Moretti as quickly as the snow had fallen from the grey sky. The worst man possible to love.

He wasn't like the boy she'd grown up with who had suddenly wanted more from life than she could give. This was a man who thrived on his playboy reputation, who was probably even now planning his next meaningless affair.

He didn't love her. She had to remember that as they left this place. For him it had been nothing more than an opportune affair, just as it should have been for her.

No matter how her heart broke at the prospect, she was determined to say goodbye in a cool and dignified way. She couldn't risk him knowing how she felt, not when he would merely dismiss that love as nothing. She would walk away from this with her head held high.

Xavier put their cases into the back of the four-wheel drive his friend had organised, thankful that they would at least be heading back to London before the end of the day. He didn't think he could spend another night here and not go to Tilly.

He glanced at her as she got into the back and wondered how she really felt. The driver sat solemnly waiting as he climbed up into the back beside her. There wouldn't be any chance of talk now. Not real talk. He'd never know if it had been simply lust-filled passion or something more that had filled their nights.

Her cold acceptance and obvious relief at being rescued proved what she'd said as they'd walked in the snow yesterday morning. Their first night together had been wrong, a mistake. So what did that make last night? Another item ticked off her list, one to prove her new-found spontaneity?

He tried to ignore the sizzle from being close to her. Tilly pulled out her phone and sent a text. She looked up at him, as if sensing his scrutiny.

'Just letting Vanessa know I'm heading back to London. We'll catch up at her party.' Her face looked a little pale but she smiled brightly at him, her excitement for her friend showing clearly. Or was it that they were on their way home and she would be free of him?

He looked out at the passing countryside, white and unrecognisable, admitting that whatever strange emotion she'd evoked in him, he wasn't looking for any kind of commitment. How could he when most nights the accident filled his dreams and the pain remained in his legs as a constant reminder. The last two nights had been dream-free. He stifled a growl of anger. He didn't deserve the love of a woman when he'd deprived another of the man she loved because of the need to win a race.

Finally the snowy countryside gave way to suburban scenes and he knew there wouldn't be much longer to endure this feeling of being tortured. He'd say goodbye, make it clear it was exactly that and walk away. Whatever he was beginning to feel for her, she deserved better.

'Not long now,' she said, her soft words dragging him from his thoughts. He didn't recognise the streets they were in and tried not to notice where they were going. He didn't want to know where she lived.

'It's good to be back,' he lied, hoping the harshness of his words would leave her in no doubt it was over between them. This was his way of protecting them both from the hot passion and tender love they'd shared that could never be repeated.

'Yes. It is.' Her soft voice held a hint of regret.

The driver pulled over and before he'd had a chance to stop himself he looked out at the street they were in. Damn. He didn't want to see its name, didn't want it imprinted on his mind so he could imagine her here. He wanted it to remain just an anonymous London street. He needed to keep her for ever in the snowy manor, in his memory at least.

'I'll walk you to your door.' He was out of the vehicle before she could argue and as he pulled her case out she joined him.

'There's no need Xavier, please.' The defiant lift of her chin reminded him of the first time he'd wanted to kiss her.

The firmness of her words also held a warning. She didn't want to prolong them being together at all, or for him to know exactly where she lived.

'*Va bene*. Then I say goodbye and thank you.'

'Thank you?' Her soft lips parted, unwittingly inviting his kiss, and he clenched his hands tightly against the need to take that kiss.

'It was a very memorable New Year's Eve, despite the circumstances that forced us together.' He knew he sounded brisk and indifferent, he could see the shock in her eyes, but he was reminding himself he couldn't have more.

'We're back in London now and our time at the manor stays there. Remember?' There was a slight wobble to her voice and a question in her eyes. He fought hard against the urge to tell her that he wanted more, if only guilt would set him free, but he couldn't tell her. She'd calmly told him he was nothing more than a tick on her list. A fling to get over the man who'd broken her heart.

'*Sì, cara*. I remember. *Arrivederci*, Natalie.' Pride kept him from saying anything—and fear of rejection.

'Goodbye, Signor Moretti.' Tilly's legs were weak as she stood there, looking into the handsome face of the man she loved. She wanted to tell him not to go, tell him something special had started, something they shouldn't let go of, but the fierce glitter in his eyes kept her words from forming.

He hadn't hidden the fact that all he'd expected had been a brief affair, company during the hours of darkness. She'd used the same excuse herself, but it had been a way of justifying how he'd swept her away that first moment their eyes had met. She'd labelled it a bucket list fling in her mind, one Jason had pushed her into. But if she was honest she knew it was more.

She picked up her small overnight bag and clutched the dress she'd draped over her arm as if it were a lifeline. Never again could she wear it, or even look at it.

She turned and walked towards the main door of her flat. The building was familiar and should have steadied her nerves, but it didn't. Nothing in London seemed to have changed—but she had.

'Tilly?'

Hope flared to life inside her at the tentative tone of his voice as she turned back to look at him. Tell me, she thought as she watched various emotions cross his face. Tell me you want me—that you've fallen in love with me.

'Yes?' Her voice sounded amazingly firm considering all that was rushing around in her head.

'Email me with the bill—and make sure the cost reflects all the time you were at the manor.'

She swallowed down the bad taste that had sprung to her lips. He didn't want her—all he was worried about was settling his bill. And she thought she'd used him.

She nodded, not able to say anything. The hard expression on his face told her he wouldn't want her to. All he wanted was to get away as fast as possible. Even now he was turning and walking back towards the car.

Before a single tear sprang from her eyes she made her way to her flat, wanting to get inside and shut him out of her life for good. Behind her she heard a car door slam shut and an engine start. The man she loved was leaving. She wanted to turn, wanted to catch one last glimpse of him, but that would only intensify her pain.

She'd got what she wanted. The opportunity to move on from Jason, to be a different woman. What she hadn't planned on doing was falling in love with a man who could leave and never give her a second thought.

She put her key in the lock, the first step to returning to her normal life. A soft whisper slipped from her lips. *'Arrivederci*, Xavier.'

CHAPTER ELEVEN

XAVIER HAD REPLAYED Tilly's parting words over and over in his head all night, her voice soft and barely above a whisper. Then her eyes had met his, hardness he'd never seen in hers making them resemble ice.

He could still feel the finality inside him, the realisation that what he'd discovered with her was over, that nothing more would ever come of those three nights they'd spent at the manor. He couldn't tell her he didn't want to see her again, that he still carried guilt from the accident and didn't deserve what he saw in her eyes. Instead, he'd used her favoured shield of professionalism, asking for her bill.

The chauffeur-driven car pulled out into London's afternoon traffic heading for the airport. He sat back and thought of Paulo's widow and the charity event she was holding tonight in Milan and knew he couldn't go. He couldn't leave London, leave Tilly. Last night he'd done nothing but think of her and knew he wanted more than a brief affair. He wanted the forever she secretly craved. But did she want it with him? He had to know.

He had to see Tilly, had to tell her he wanted her in his life. He couldn't allow guilt to rule him any longer, because if those three nights at the manor had been the start of something special he couldn't let it pass him by. She'd helped him find peace and had begun to free him from the guilt he'd carried since the accident. But more importantly—he loved her.

He pulled out his phone and dialled. 'Sofia,' he said calmly as Paulo's widow answered, then spoke firmly in Italian. 'I'm not going to be able to get there this evening. Can you forgive me?'

'Is it the woman you were snowed in with?'

'How do you know that?' Suspicion narrowed his eyes and the urge to confide in her was overwhelming.

'Your emails were full of her. Go to her, Xavier. You've punished yourself long enough. Paulo would want you to be happy and so do I.' Sofia's firm words lifted the fog that had clouded his mind and he knew exactly what he had to do.

After wishing her luck for that evening, he ended the call. 'Change of plan,' he said to the driver, and instructed him first to go to a jeweller's in Knightsbridge then to Tilly's address, the one that was emblazoned on his memory.

Impatience and apprehension filled him as the car turned around and negotiated the heavy traffic. All he could think of was Tilly. But would she see him? He had to make her understand he couldn't accept her goodbye. He couldn't walk away.

During those dark hours at the manor, as the blizzard had raged, they'd shared their innermost vulnerabilities and were now inexplicably connected—whether they liked it or not.

A short while later he stood on the street where they'd said goodbye and thought of the vulnerable woman he'd held in his arms as darkness had shrouded them. He let out a deep breath. The evening darkness of January was beginning to descend. It was as if he'd been transported back to that night in front of the fire, the night Tilly had exposed every vulnerable emotion he could possibly feel. Each one was with him now, some urging him on, forcing him to cross the road to her flat and knock on the door. Others held him back. But none of them could be ignored any longer. He wanted

Tilly, not just with lust and passion but with something much deeper and more profound.

He didn't believe she'd only wanted a brief fling. How could what they'd shared have been so intense if that was really true? He cursed the fact he hadn't challenged her or told her he didn't want to say goodbye. Just as he hoped she had been doing, he'd hidden behind the fear of rejection—but he couldn't do that any longer. Paulo's widow had made him realise that.

Tilly watched from the window as Xavier stood on the street, his indecision clear, before he crossed the street and made his way to the main door of her flat. Her heart thumped hard and memories of those blissful nights at the manor rushed back from the place she'd locked them. She'd successfully done that, but now his unexpected presence made her wonder what would have happened if she and Xavier had been forced to stay in the manor longer.

He would have tired of her within days and she wouldn't have been able to hide her love, something he wasn't capable of. That night in front of the fire she'd tried to heal his pain, tried to love him, but all he'd wanted had been to get away as fast as he could.

What did he want from her now? In an act of self-preservation she'd made it quite clear what had happened between them had meant nothing and would never be repeated.

Judging by the internet pictures she'd seen of him out last night—hours after they'd said goodbye, with a very beautiful woman hanging on his arm and every word—he had moved on. Forgotten her completely. It was what she'd wanted, but it didn't make it any easier. She loved him, had missed him next to her at night.

The need to know more of Xavier, to see his handsome face again, had made her do the one thing she'd never done before—look up a man on the internet. Not just as a professional check for business purposes but because she'd had to.

Initially she'd been looking for information on the accident, wanting to know why he blamed himself, and had found nothing to suggest anyone had blamed him. Then with one final click she had stumbled across photos of him looking more than comfortable with a new woman at a celebrity party. Pain had slashed through her. Hurt, betrayal and finally resignation. He would never look at her in any other way than for a casual affair.

At least now she could understand his haste to get away from the manor. Not only did he regret their intimacy, he'd moved on, his next conquest waiting in the wings.

Her doorbell rang, distracting her from the painful thoughts, and with a heavy heart she pressed the button to open the main door of her flat. It was time to be brave, move forward and not look back. She couldn't let Xavier know that being with him had made her realise she'd never loved Jason, or that he'd stirred her childhood memories as well as her heart, and that as soon as she'd returned home she'd set about contacting her father's family in Tuscany, ticking off another item on her list.

Now they wanted to meet her. She should be ecstatic, but her elation was tinged with sadness. She'd wanted to tell Xavier, thank him for giving her that final push, that final bit of courage. Her bag was packed and she was leaving at the weekend, but first she had a night out with Vanessa.

That thought lifted her spirits a little, even though Vanessa had grilled her constantly about this mysterious Italian with whom she'd spent an entire three days locked away from the world. After a bit of pressure she'd told Vanessa that she'd ticked an item off her list, that she'd moved on from Jason, but she couldn't admit she'd fallen in love and given him her virginity, something Vanessa had had no idea had still existed. Not when the man in question was even more capable of breaking her heart than Jason had been.

A loud knock on her flat door jolted her from her thoughts and she looked through the viewer to see Xavier, his back to the door, impatience in his stance as he waited for her to open it. There was no mistaking who he was. She'd know that rigid set of Xavier's shoulders anywhere. They, along with everything else about him, were imprinted on her mind for evermore.

She pushed her hands through her hair and took a deep breath. She had no idea what he wanted, but it wasn't her. She took in a deep breath, preparing to face the man she loved.

'Xavier,' she said as she opened the door, injecting a happy note into her voice, one she was far from feeling. 'We agreed. Remember?'

As soon as she'd said the words, she knew she'd given herself away. The way he coolly assessed her sent her nerves jangling and she resisted the urge to give in to the need to babble on. She didn't have to explain herself to anyone, least of all Xavier Moretti.

'*Sì, mi ricordo.*' His brisk tone left her in no doubt he wasn't here to rekindle the passion they'd shared. 'May I come in?'

The piercing intensity in his eyes sent exasperation rushing through her, but she bit back her retort. If he thought he could come from one woman back to her, then he had got it drastically wrong. Just as she had done, trusting him at the manor. 'I am rather busy packing.'

He looked surprised and she couldn't help the smile that tugged at her lips. 'Where and when are you going?' The firmness in his voice couldn't hide the shock her news had given him.

'I'm going to Tuscany to meet my father's family.'

'Something else crossed off your list?' The hard look in his eyes made a chill run down her spine.

She nodded. 'I have you to thank for that.' It was true. If he hadn't made her talk about the past, unlocking a door she'd hidden behind like a terrified animal, then she wouldn't be going. She wouldn't even have contacted them.

'And when would this be?'

She stood back, giving in to the need to see him again. He walked past her and into the small flat she proudly called home, only too aware it would be inferior to what he would be used to—but he was in her world now. He glanced at her passport and boarding pass, which sat neatly on her kitchen counter. 'This Saturday?'

'Yes.' She resented the fact that he'd helped himself to the information, realising he was now very different from the relaxed man she'd shared a few passionate nights with. He might be in her world, but he'd brought his own agenda with him. 'What is it you want, Xavier?'

Unexplainably irritated by his presence, she glared at him, wanting to know why he was there, but another part of her dreaded the answer, especially after seeing last night's internet photos.

'We need to talk.' He moved a step closer and it was all she could do not to move away. She stayed firm and lifted her chin a little, looking directly into his handsome face, noting the hint of stubble and realising that even at the manor, when everything had been so different, he'd been clean-shaven. As she looked more closely she saw lines of tiredness etched on his face.

'There's nothing to say, Xavier.'

'You know part of the story, now I want you to know the rest.'

Why was he talking to her like this? Cautiously, allowing a bit of hope into her heart, she responded, 'Go on.'

'Christmas wasn't something I celebrated, not after destroying Paulo's family.' His face hardened, all trace of humour gone. Whatever it was that had happened at the racetrack that day haunted him still.

'So why the New Year dinner party?' She sensed there was more but knew he wouldn't tell her. He hadn't when she'd asked about his aversion to Christmas at the manor. She had been kept behind his defensive wall.

'The New Year dinner party was for the benefit of my parents. Nothing more.' His dark gaze met hers and she saw confusion and honesty in them. 'An item crossed off *my* list.'

She touched his arm and those intense dark eyes searched her face. 'I think you're being too hard on yourself. You're punishing yourself when you shouldn't.'

'Because of me and my need to win that race, my friend is dead. I had to be hard on myself.' The words snapped from him and the pain in his voice froze the air around them before shattering it.

'I don't know much about motorcycle racing, Xavier, but I do know accidents are investigated and reports are made.' She tried to placate him, tried to smooth the pain. They might be in her small flat, back in the real world, but right now it was as if the magic that had caught them in its grip at the manor had returned, weaving around them, shutting everything out.

'I don't need a damn report to tell me it was my fault. I know that, here.' He thumped his fist against his chest, the pain in that action evident.

She wanted to reach for him, to wrap her arms around him and let her love wash away all that misplaced guilt, all that self-inflicted pain, but something held her back. She still didn't understand why he was there. Why now when he'd only just been in the company of a new woman?

'I saw it on the internet, Xavier.' The words were a firm whisper, severing the thread of connection that had just woven itself around them. 'Nobody blames you.'

Xavier stood and looked at Tilly, her blonde hair falling around her shoulders, and he remembered how it had felt, how soft it had been as he'd slid his fingers into it before kissing her.

'You looked it up?'

Her gorgeous blue eyes widened in shock and she drew in a quick breath, but she didn't move. After what felt like an eternity she finally spoke again, her voice holding an unsteady quiver. 'Yes.'

'And what did you decide?' This was his worst fear. She blamed him, believed he was guilty. Why else would she look him up on the internet?

'That you are being too hard on yourself.' Firmness entered her voice and as he looked into her eyes he could see determination there and a strength he'd never noticed before. Her words echoed Sofia's.

He realised that right now he had the biggest fight of his life on his hands. The fight for the woman he loved, the woman he wanted in his life for evermore. This was worse than being on the track, pushing the bike harder and faster to win. If he lost this fight, he'd lose everything.

'Why are you here?' The sharp question fired at him, dragging him from his thoughts, focusing his attention on what he was there for—the woman he loved.

'To talk to you.' It was all he could do not to reach for her, not to draw her close and kiss the surprise from her beautiful face, but already he could see her backing away emotionally. She was slipping behind the wall she'd built to keep everyone out and he couldn't let that happen.

'Why? It won't serve any purpose.' She stepped away from him, trying to put as much distance as possible between them. For the first time in his adult life he was unsure how to read a woman's actions, especially as he still hadn't worked out what he was going to say. All he knew was that he'd had to say something.

'We are no longer strangers, Tilly. *Dio mio*, we have spent two nights in each other's arms like lovers.'

Lovers. The word raced in his head. He hadn't wanted to love her, but it had happened and now all he wanted was her love. She'd touched something deep inside him. She had changed and healed him.

When it had happened he didn't know, but it had. He recalled the first moment he'd seen her standing in the courtyard at Wimble Manor as the snow had drifted to the ground around her, landing on her red woolly hat, which he'd found so very amusing. Had that been the moment?

'No, Xavier. We agreed. Those nights meant nothing.' Was she really dismissing what they'd shared as nothing?

That first moment her lips had met his rushed back. He was there once more, standing by the Christmas tree, loaded tension swirling around them, dragging them deeper and deeper under the spell of love.

Now that spell was no longer. The harsh glitter in her eyes didn't hold any softness, any love. If anything, they held contempt.

'It doesn't have to stay that way.' He moved towards her but she stepped back.

'It does, Xavier. You are not the type of man I need. You would never make me happy. We have to say goodbye.'

He frowned, trying to process her words. 'Goodbye?'

'Yes, goodbye.' She stood firmly in the middle of her living room, glaring angrily at him. What had changed in such a short time? 'So, if you don't mind, I'd like you to leave.'

CHAPTER TWELVE

TILLY'S HEART BROKE as she stood there, knee deep in deception. She had to be strong, had to keep her emotions under control, anything that would stop her going to him, throwing her arms around his neck and herself at the mercy of the love she had for him. Love that had overshadowed every other emotion she'd experienced in those few days at the manor.

What had happened over the New Year had been deeper than the passion, more addictive than the sensual feel of his touch. It had also happened with such speed it seemed impossible, but there was no doubt. Not any more. She'd fallen in love with a man who'd been looking for nothing more than a distraction to while away the hours of being snowbound at New Year.

'There isn't a future for us, Xavier, there never was.' She kept her voice devoid of emotion as his eyes narrowed. He was watching every move she made. Did he suspect she wasn't telling him the truth?

'Do you seriously expect me to believe that?' He moved towards her, his voice heavily accented and becoming softer. 'When you were a virgin?'

Stunned, she could only look at him, knowing the truth of his words. She'd given herself to him, believing, even though they didn't have a future, there wasn't anyone else in their lives. It had meant so little to him he'd gone straight to the arms of another woman.

'Believe what you like. There isn't a future for us. You never wanted what we shared to continue. Now, if you don't mind, I'd like you to leave.'

She moved towards the front door, desperate for him to leave. All she wanted to do was give in to her grief. The man she loved would never love her. She'd been nothing more than entertainment on a cold winter night. If his family had arrived as planned there was no way she and Xavier would have spent the night together.

'No, Natalie.' He spoke firmly but still managed to caress her name, taunting her with the use of it. She closed her eyes against the memories that soft and seductive tone released. She couldn't remember now. She had to be brave and strong. *'Lo non lascio.'*

Tilly's heart sank. Did he have to use his first language? She tried to think through the fog of confusion, trying to recall her childhood Italian. He wasn't leaving. Well, she wasn't going to stand here and be tormented by him.

'You will leave. Right now.' She folded her arms, whether to protect her heart or stop herself from reaching for him she wasn't sure.

Xavier moved towards her, his dark eyes intense. They made her feel as if she was the only woman in the world he wanted. But she knew that wasn't true. 'I don't want to leave you, Tilly.'

Please, she wanted to shout as he spoke again in Italian. It sounded so romantic, so seductive, but she knew it wouldn't mean what she wanted it to—that he wanted her, loved her.

She was so distraught by his presence that she couldn't fathom the fast-flowing words, couldn't decide what he'd been saying. All she knew was that he had to leave. Right now.

'Just go, Xavier. I don't want to hear what you have to say, no matter what language you use.' She turned her back on him and strode to the window, looking out over the grey London street.

* * *

Xavier walked to the door of Tilly's flat, total desolation filling him. He'd almost poured his heart out. Unable to think in English, he'd told her in Italian, which he knew she could understand, that he was not going to walk away from the woman he loved. But her insistence that he leave had numbed him, making speaking in any language impossible. She'd even turned her back on him.

He couldn't go. He couldn't leave her. Sofia's advice drove him on and he strode over to where she stood, resolutely staring out. 'I'm not going anywhere, Natalie, not without saying what I have to say about us.'

She turned to look at him, her face upturned and the blue of her eyes so vivid it was like being at sea on a summer day. 'There is no us. Never has been and never will be. I was your hired help. We should never have done what we did. It was wrong. Wrong on every level.'

'Not after the stroke of midnight on New Year's Eve, you weren't my hired help. And what is so wrong with passion?'

'Nothing.'

He narrowed his eyes as she looked up at him, defiance in every breath she took. She was so beautiful he wanted to lower his head and claim her lips once more, to bring that passion back to life until it consumed them completely.

'Then why hide from it? Why don't you allow it into your life? What are you afraid of, Tilly?'

He touched her arm in a gesture of concern but she flinched and stepped back from him. He was losing her—and he couldn't let that happen. He couldn't lose the only woman he had ever loved. The only woman he would ever love.

'You are the one hiding, not me,' she said calmly, and frustration zipped around his body. He'd never thought telling a woman he loved her would be so difficult.

Her words were true. He was hiding, or rather avoiding the issue. He knew he was sidestepping the moment he had to put his heart on the line and tell her he loved her, that he couldn't live without her. He would be exposing all his vulnerabilities, exposing himself to her rejection. Was that why he couldn't form the words in English? Because he knew for certain she would understand?

'I'm not hiding from anything.'

'All the time you were at the manor you hated the Christmas tree and everything it represented. If I'm hiding from passion then you too are hiding from something.'

'You are right,' he said, and let out a deep breath. She had to know everything, from the nightmares that haunted his sleep to the love he felt for her. He had to tell her now, because he sensed this was the last time he would ever see her, that if he didn't say something now she would shut him out of her life completely— and he wasn't about to stand by and allow that. 'Maybe we should talk over dinner?'

'No.' She shook her head determinedly.

'*Ottimo.* We shall talk now.'

She didn't move away from the window and when she returned her attention to the rainy street his heart sank. She didn't want to hear what he had to say.

'It's time for me to move on, to start living my life again.' The fact that he could do that was all down to her, but he couldn't do it without her.

She looked earnestly into his face, her blue eyes searching his. 'You're right. You bear the scars, both physically and emotionally. You've lost a friend, but he wouldn't want you to put your life on hold.'

He frowned at her as she said almost the same as Sofia had. 'No, he wouldn't.'

'Would you want that if the roles were reversed? Would you want him to live with guilt eating at him for the rest of his life?'

'That is what Sofia, his widow, has just told me. She doesn't blame me and said Paulo would be angry if he knew I was.' Images of his friend rushed through his mind.

'So now you can stop punishing yourself.'

'The way I handled those days at the manor was wrong, but I can't lose you, Tilly.' He put himself on the line as he said the words. She didn't move. It looked as if his words had frozen her. 'Not when I love you.'

He'd finally said it. He'd given life to the emotion that had been burning deep inside him since the moment he'd met Tilly. The silence that filled the room was so loud it almost deafened him.

Tilly's head spun and her heart thumped harder in her chest. She looked into Xavier's eyes, hoping to see love, but saw only hard determination. How could he say he loved her when he had just returned from another woman's side?

'You don't mean that.' She shook her head in denial and returned her gaze to the growing darkness of the street outside, wishing he would stop torturing her. He'd been photographed with another woman—hours after leaving her.

He took hold of her arms and spun her round to look at him. She wanted to avert her gaze, but with the heat of his touch burning through her jumper she couldn't. 'I mean every word of it, Tilly. I have thought of nothing else but you since the moment we met.'

She lowered her gaze, trying to resist the urge to babble out whatever words came into her head, but the urge was too strong. 'But I saw you—at the party last night, with your latest lover.'

His grasp on her arms loosened and she knew she'd said the wrong thing. 'How?'

Now she would have to spill the whole sorry truth about looking him up on the internet, about searching for information about the accident. 'I saw the pictures on the internet.' She pressed her lips firmly together to prevent herself airing more babbling excuses.

She kept her gaze averted but when she looked up again it was to see a wary look of surprise on his handsome face. 'Does that mean you couldn't stop thinking of me?'

'Yes. I mean no.' She knew she was in danger of talking too much again and pulled herself free of his grasp. She couldn't think straight when he was so near, when the intoxicating scent of him made her remember those nights she'd sworn she would forget.

'Natalie, don't.' The sexy accent he used for her name drew her up sharply and those memories hurtled back.

'Don't what?' she asked in exasperation. He really had to go before she spilled everything out and told him she loved him. But she couldn't do that. She couldn't risk it. Already he'd tired of her and could hurt her far more than Jason ever had. She couldn't face rejection again.

'Don't hide. Don't run.'

She couldn't look at him. 'I'm not hiding or running, Xavier. I just want to be honest with myself and you. I can't be with you, not how you want anyway.'

'And how exactly do I want to be with you?' The gruffness of his voice hinted at his frustration.

'I can't be just another woman, one you call when you are in London. I'm not that type of girl.'

He took her swiftly in his arms, pulling her excruciatingly close to him. 'I've tried to forget you, tried to put you to the back of my mind as nothing more than a memory. I have no idea who I was pictured with. I might have been there at the party, but in my mind I was still at the manor with you, the only woman I want.'

Suddenly everything became clear and Xavier could see why Tilly was so anxious. Since the accident he'd never had a serious relationship. He'd only dated a woman once, always avoiding anything more intimate, worried about his scarred body.

'I see my recently acquired reputation has coloured your view of me.' He didn't know how to explain without scaring her away completely. All he knew was that he had to tell her.

'Something like that, yes,' she said, and locked back up into his face. He wanted to lower his lips to hers and kiss her to prove she was the only woman he wanted. Could a kiss prove how much he loved her? The whole concept of love was totally new to him. Her eyelashes lowered over her eyes as she looked down, the long dark lashes sweeping against the pale skin in an alluring way.

'I was drowning in guilt and badly scarred. What woman would seriously want me? You are the only woman I have made love to since the accident.' Each word was raw, pulling at his heart as if being ripped from it, dragging out emotions he'd kept locked away, preferring guilt and self-pity. 'I wanted you so badly, Tilly.'

'You did?' The soft whisper caught his attention and he lifted her chin with his thumb and finger, forcing her to look directly at him. The blue of her eyes was shrouded in tears threatening to fall and he hated it that he'd made her cry.

But she wasn't fighting any more. She wasn't resisting what had sprung to life between them the very first moment their eyes had met. She was here in his arms—exactly where he wanted her to be. Those two huskily whispered words whirled round in his head.

'You are the only woman I ever wanted to stay after finding out about the accident, because you are the only woman I want. I love you, Natalie Rogers, and I intend to love you more each and every single day for the rest of my life—if you will let me.'

'I want to say yes.' She looked at him, a tear slipping from first one eye then the other. He caught them with his finger, wiped them away, cursing softly because he'd made her cry.

'But what?' He sensed the doubt, the reservations she was fighting.

'Jason breaking things off was my fault. I didn't want passion and he didn't want only companionship.' She looked down again, as if she was gathering her strength. When she looked back up her blue eyes glittered. 'I can't be who I was those two nights at the manor. That wasn't me. Nothing seemed real then.'

'Our passion was real.' How could she deny that sexy and passionate woman had been her? Every time she'd caressed him she'd set light to him. Every time he'd touched her the intensity of it had risen.

'Because we were different people, cut off from reality. I can't give you passion and excitement, just as I couldn't give it to Jason. I'm scared to.'

Anger simmered to the fore. Damn that man. 'What are you scared of?'

It wasn't making any sense. She'd given herself to him with passionate abandon. What had burned between them those two nights had been so hot it still fired his body now to think of it.

'Loving and losing.'

'Losing?'

'My parents,' she said quietly. 'The love they had for one another was so all-consuming. They only had eyes for each other, but it didn't stop them being wrenched apart. It didn't stop my mother's heart breaking after my father died.'

'Natalie, Natalie.' He pulled her against him, holding her tight and kissing her hair. He closed his eyes against the pain she must have felt as a child. A fluid flow of Italian left his lips and she pulled back to look up at him, her eyes moist with unshed tears.

'I can't be like that,' she whispered softly. He knew then she hadn't been able to love Jason because she'd been scared of the consequences. Joy at knowing she hadn't loved the man she should have married, that she didn't love him now, surged through him.

'You don't have to be.' He lowered his lips to hers, brushing his over the plumpness of hers and enjoying the sensation that fizzed to life. 'All I want is the woman who arrived at the manor, full of joy at the falling snow as I stood and watched her from the doorway. You just need to be you. The woman I love.'

'Do you really mean that?' Hope shone in her eyes and in his heart simultaneously.

'I want you in my life always, Natalie. I want to be with you as you rediscover your family. I want you to be my wife.'

Her gorgeous eyes widened and he laughed

gently as he placed another light kiss on her lips. 'Your wife?'

'Yes, Tilly, my wife, and to prove it I will do it properly.' He stepped back from her, reached into his pocket as he lowered himself to one knee. He took hold of her hand in one of his and held the ring box out to her. '*Mi vuoi sposare*, Natalie?'

'But we've only just met.' Despite the protest, she was smiling.

'*Sì*, and by next Christmas Eve we will be back at the manor for our wedding. There will be the biggest and most brightly decorated tree possible—and our families, so we won't be quite so alone.'

She took the ring from the box, a smile of wonder on her face, and he stood up and slipped it on her finger. It fitted perfectly. Yet another sign that they too fitted perfectly together.

'*Sì, lo ti sposerò*, Xavier.' Her acceptance in Italian warmed his heart more than anything and he crushed her to him with a demanding kiss. The woman he loved was going to be his wife.

EPILOGUE

TRUE TO HIS WORD, Xavier rented Wimble Manor for the next Christmas, requesting the biggest and most brightly decorated tree possible. He couldn't believe how lucky he was to have Tilly in his life and he looked at her as she entered the grand hallway. The wedding dress she wore was beautiful and the faux fur-lined hood of the cape framed her face, one that shone with happiness as she looked at him.

This time last year he had hated Christmas and anything to do with it. He'd thought he didn't deserve to marry and settle down, but now he knew he'd just been waiting for Tilly to waltz into his life.

'Hi,' his beautiful bride whispered, as she joined him where he waited for her among their close friends and family. There was a nervous tremor in her voice and he knew it was after what had happened almost two years ago, but there was no possible way he was going to turn his back on her. How could he when he loved her so completely?

'*Sei bellissima.*' He took the tips of her fingers and raised them to his lips, not taking his eyes from her once as a blush crept over her cheeks. 'You didn't bring the snow with you this time?'

She smiled up at him and whispered mischievously, 'Not yet.'

Tilly's heart swelled as her new husband kissed her for the first time. They were standing at the bottom of the stairs, next to a fantastically decorated tree that held pride of place in the centre of the large hallway. Exactly the same spot they had first shared a kiss and where Xavier had arranged for them to be married.

Around them applause sounded and she turned shyly to see her mother, her father's brother and his family and Vanessa, her maid of honour. It was a perfect day and soon it would be followed by a more than perfect night in the arms of the man she loved so tenderly yet so passionately.

There was a tinge of sadness because she would be leaving behind her mother and her best friend when she and Xavier moved to Italy in the New Year, but wherever he went she would go too. It was hard to recall that last Christmas had been so lonely and now, just one year later, she was married to the man of her dreams.

She smiled up at him. 'Thank you,' she whispered, and his brows quirked in that sexy kind of way she'd come to adore.

'What for, *mia cara*?'

'For arranging all this. When you told me you would organise the wedding, I never imagined this.'

'Wimble Manor is where I first met you, where I first fell in love.' He lowered his voice so their wedding guests wouldn't hear. 'And where we first made love. It will always be a special place.'

'I wish we were alone like that again.'

He pressed his lips to hers, sending a shiver of awareness down her spine. 'Soon, my beautiful bride, soon. Once our guests have gone, it can snow for as long as it likes.'

* * * * *